"You Don't Know Anything About Me!

I came to this fund raiser with Russ because his mission in life hasn't been protecting his millions from women like me."

"Women like you?" Clay repeated.

"Now you're catching on. I'm the hired help! I cater parties like this for the privilege of putting food in my mouth. I do it for the luxury of paying my rent. So tell me, Clay—how do you feel about me now?"

BEVERLY BIRD

currently makes her home in Arizona, though she spent most of her life on a small island off the coast of New Jersey. She is devoted to both her husband and her writing but still makes time for travel and horse-back riding.

Dear Reader:

SILHOUETTE DESIRE is an exciting new line of contemporary romances from Silhouette Books. During the past year, many Silhouette readers have written in telling us what other types of stories they'd like to read from Silhouette, and we've kept these comments and suggestions in mind in developing SILHOUETTE DESIRE.

DESIREs feature all of the elements you like to see in a romance, plus a more sensual, provocative story. So if you want to experience all the excitement, passion and joy of falling in love, then SILHOUETTE DESIRE is for you.

Karen Solem
Editor-in-Chief
Silhouette Books

BEVERLY BIRD
Fool's Gold

Silhouette Desire
Published by Silhouette Books New York
America's Publisher of Contemporary Romance

Silhouette Books by Beverly Bird

Emeralds in the Dark (IM #3)
The Fires of Winter (IM #23)
The Best Reasons (DES #190)
Fool's Gold (DES #209)

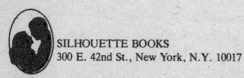

SILHOUETTE BOOKS
300 E. 42nd St., New York, N.Y. 10017

Copyright © 1985 by Beverly Bird

Distributed by Pocket Books

ISBN: 0-373-05209-X

First Silhouette Books printing May, 1985

10 9 8 7 6 5 4 3 2 1

America's Publisher of Contemporary Romance

Printed in the U.S.A.

For my "live-in" editor and husband, Steve,
and my "real" editor, Leslie Wainger,
both of whose judgment infallibly
picks up where mine leaves off.
Thanks.

Fool's
Gold

1

He was the last person in the world she wanted to see. If Devon Jordan had made a list of all the people she hoped wouldn't attend the Myers' lavish cocktail party that evening, Clayton Wyatt would have topped it. She'd considered the possibility, of course, but then she'd discarded it as a paranoid worry. Clay Wyatt didn't attend many parties.

But he was at this one. Devon tightened her grip on the plate of caviar canapés she held to keep from dropping them. Her limbs, even her fingers, suddenly felt weak. Acting without thinking, she backed quickly into the shadows of the door to keep him from spotting her. The surprise of seeing him again made her heart skip a single beat, then leap into a panicky fluttering.

He leaned insolently against the baby grand in the corner of the living room, nursing a neat Scotch as he surveyed the room. His eyes were as she remembered them, pale green chips of ice. Now they looked slightly bored and mocking as he assessed the people gathered in the Myers' opulent home. The very way he stood there told anyone who looked at him that he neither wanted nor needed their attention. His partial smile was vaguely cynical, his looks classically handsome. His hair was thick and tawny with a touch of gray at the temples—just a bit more than she remembered. But then, a whole year had passed since she had last seen him.

It seemed more like yesterday, she mused, pressing her free hand against her chest in a vain effort to still her heart. She had still been married that night a year before when she attended Moira and Derrick Kendall's private benefit for the Phoenix Symphony. Her life had been vastly different then. The diamond choker she had worn that night had long since been sold. She had no idea where Ian, her ex-husband, was now or what had become of him. As things turned out, she had ended up leaving him within a week of the benefit. He had supposedly been out of town on business the night of that party. In actuality, he was in Las Vegas—just as he had been several times a month for six years—gambling away the sizable inheritance she had brought into their marriage and wining and dining the woman he had been having an affair with during the entire time Devon was married to him.

But what Ian had done to her, to her feeling of pride and self-worth, was neither here nor there, she reminded herself. She brushed her ex-husband from her thoughts and peeked around the doorway to steal another look at the quite different man who was still leaning against the piano. The bottom line was that, under different circumstances, she would have given her right arm to run into Clay Wyatt again. Yet now that it had finally happened, she couldn't bring herself to approach him. Her guilt, her embarrassment, wouldn't let her. Her first meeting with him still lived too vividly in her memory.

Tall, lean, and agile-looking, impeccably dressed, he snagged her attention that night almost immediately. He was lounging in a chair near Moira's French doors, watching her steadily. Devon could still feel the tingle of excitement that had skittered down her spine every time she looked up and met his eye.

It was odd that she didn't know him. The endless parties and gatherings she attended invariably included the same small circle of Phoenician entrepreneurs and their wives. A new face was a rarity. But Clay's face was new, at least to Devon, and his shimmering green eyes never seemed to leave her. She had felt herself flushing and gradually losing her composure as her gaze was drawn to him again and again. It was as though he was silently calling to her, but she didn't know him, had never laid eyes on him before in her life.

His presence electrified the air, but no one other than Devon seemed to notice how warm and close the room was becoming. Finally, her nerves rattled, she left to find the bar and dropped a few extra ice cubes into her bourbon. She kept her eyes on the door as she took several nervous sips, half expecting the stranger to follow her and appear there. When minutes passed and he hadn't, her nerves started to sing with almost unbearable anticipation.

She placed her glass emphatically on the bar again and slipped outside through yet another set of French doors. The faintly cool December air felt like heaven as it soothed her feverish skin. Then she left the patio and headed down toward the stables behind the house. Derrick's sleek thoroughbreds were his pride and joy, and they fascinated Devon. She never visited her best friend and her husband without taking a minute to see their horses. Tonight, they offered her a perfect opportunity to slip away from the party. She wasn't able to keep herself from wondering if the stranger would slip away as well.

Southern Dancer, a petite filly and one of the few horses that wasn't so skittish that Devon couldn't get near her, was still in the paddock. Devon cast a quick look over her shoulder at the brightly lit house and grinned impishly. Never one to stand on ceremony, she hiked up her long skirt until it swirled about her thighs; then, clutching a handful of white satin in one hand, she fumbled with the lock on the gate with the other.

"My, what lovely legs you have."

The strong male voice floated to her through the night. Devon let go of the gate abruptly and turned around to search the darkness, her pulse pounding. It was him—it *had* to be the stranger who had been watching her. Hadn't she suspected all along that he would follow her?

Amazingly, her voice came out smooth and flippant despite the fact that her stomach churned with anticipation. "Thanks," she replied, speaking into the darkness. "I've got great eyes too. I'd tell you they were all the better to see you with, but you're doing an admirable job of hiding."

There was a soft, warm chuckle before the stranger stepped out of the shadows cast by a palm tree caught in the light of the house. He walked toward her slowly and nonchalantly, his hands deep in his pockets, his eyes pinning her to the spot. Devon's nerves tingled as she waited for him to reach her.

"I wasn't hiding," he protested mildly, his voice like velvet. "I was spying on you. You've just been caught red-handed. All I've got to do now is decide whether or not I want to turn you in."

Devon gaped at him in confusion for a split second. Ultimately, it was his slight smile that brought one to her own lips. "Turn me in? For what? Other than not being a model of decorum and flashing my legs at a horse, you haven't got a thing on me," she responded, playing along with him.

"Would you care to place a wager on that?" He relaxed against a fence post but never seemed to lose the edge of control she sensed in him. "I happen to have it on very good authority that Derrick is highly protective of his horses. If he caught you out here trying to get into the paddock, all hell would break loose."

Devon opened her mouth to tell him that she knew Derrick well enough to get away with it, but something made her words catch in her throat. She found herself savoring the feeling of anonymity and freshness the stranger brought to her. It had been so long since she had escaped the boring routine and familiar faces that dominated her life.

"You'll have to do better than that," she heard herself saying to him instead. "You can't rat on me without implicating yourself. How are you going to explain your mysterious presence at the scene of the crime?"

"No problem. I'm bigger than Derrick is. I can protect both of us from his wrath if need be. That is, if you can convince me that I ought to protect you."

The provocative innuendo in his words made her heart leap crazily. "Derrick might be small," she managed to counter nonchalantly, "but I've heard tell that he's wiry. If I were you, I'd be just a wee bit worried and a little less cocky."

The stranger's smile—never wide to begin with—tightened even more until it looked almost hard. "You can put your faith in me. I was taught to fight by one of the toughest street gangs in Chicago. I haven't had to use the know-how in quite awhile, but they tell me it's just like swimming and sex. Once you learn, you never forget."

He had watched her with an oddly speculative gaze as he finished. Devon looked away from him, feeling herself flush suddenly with inexplicable sexual excitement. He had mentioned sex as though it were any other sport, but his voice held the whisper of promise.

"Well?" he had taunted her, pulling her attention back to him. "What's it going to be? Are you going to try to convince me that I shouldn't turn you in? Tell me what you're doing out here instead of inside partaking of Moira's champagne and hors d'oeuvres. With legs like yours, I'd figure you'd be tearing up the dance floor."

Devon took a deep, steadying breath and leaned back against the fence post opposite his. Tilting her head to one side, she matched the small, amused smile that had returned to the stranger's lips. "With whom?" she countered. "As near as I can tell, there are only two unattached men here tonight. One of them is six inches

13

shorter than I am and must have a hundred and fifty pounds on me. The other is you, and all you've done is stare at me all evening."

Her words were smooth, but guilt was beginning to churn in the pit of her stomach, leaving a rancid taste in her mouth that made her smile falter. Oh, no, she thought wildly. What am I doing? I'm *married*. I can't be doing this. Try as she might to soothe her conscience by telling herself that she was merely talking to the man, it didn't work. There was a sense of anticipation and urgency in the air, an overtone to all of their words. She was flirting with him, plain and simple. The guilt was so strong that it almost sickened her. She pushed herself away from the fence post abruptly, scowling.

"Chickening out?" the stranger mocked her.

Devon stopped dead in her tracks and turned around again to stare at him. Had he read her mind? A sweet tension sang in the air between them as she met his eyes. "On what?" she asked.

"On trusting my ability to defend us against Derrick."

Her laugh was shaky. "Oh, that."

"You were thinking of something else?"

He continued to watch her with that slight, assessing smile. It was as though he knew precisely what she was thinking and dared her to voice the thought. "I—no," she began, feeling flustered. His smile lifted almost infinitesimally on one side at her answer. "Who are you, anyway?" she blurted suddenly, panic building inside her.

Both of the stranger's eyebrows lifted to match his crooked smile, but he didn't respond.

"Why haven't I seen you before?" she rushed on. "The guest lists at these parties aren't exactly varied. Why don't I know you?"

Surprise and a clear distrust flashed across the stranger's handsome features. "Don't you?" he countered bluntly.

Devon scowled again. "Would I ask if I did?"

"Maybe."

"What on earth for?" She took a step closer to him

and searched his face. Then she nodded emphatically. "I was right the first time. I don't know you. And considering the fact that you seem slightly paranoid about that, maybe it's better that I don't."

His robust laugh surprised her. "Touché," he answered, then paused. "Clayton Wyatt," he supplied after a moment.

Devon leaned back against the fence post again. "Pleased to meet you. I think." Her eyes narrowed in concentration as she continued to search his face. "Clayton Wyatt." She rolled his name around on her tongue a few more times, then her eyes widened in recognition. "Wait! I do know you! Or rather, I know about you. You're the character who owns all those hotels."

A mixture of annoyance and amusement touched his eyes. "Character?" he echoed. "Well, I've been called worse, I suppose."

She ignored his gibe as her thoughts raced. "You've got one here in Phoenix," she mused aloud. "And one in Denver and one in San Francisco . . ."

Suddenly his expression soured. "You're forgetting Los Angeles and Chicago. For someone who didn't recognize me, you've got a fair amount of the facts. I'd help you out and give you my profit and loss statement, but I don't keep the figures on the tip of my tongue."

Devon stiffened at the sudden animosity in his tone. Her eyes flashed angrily as she watched his face. It had become closed and more than a little wary.

"I'd apologize," she answered bluntly, "but I really don't know what I'd be apologizing for. If you've got some kind of hang-up regarding your identity, that's certainly not my problem. You can keep your profit and loss figures, or whatever you called them. I've never been very good with numbers anyway. I hate to break it to you, but they wouldn't mean a thing to me."

"No?" His response was partially mocking, partially speculative.

"No," she repeated flatly. "Look, I'm not at all interested in the details of your wealth. I'd have to have lived in a cave half my life not to have recognized your name. I'm just an average member of the American public. Of course I know that you're worth some outrageous amount of money. So who cares? All I was asking you was why I haven't seen you at more parties."

Some of his reserve seemed to crack. The stiff set of his broad shoulders relaxed slightly and he had the good grace to look embarrassed. Devon pushed on. "I can't see many hostesses deliberately leaving you off their guest lists. Whether you like to admit it or not, you're probably one of America's most eligible bachelors." Suddenly she laughed. It had a bright, delighted ring. "Oh, Lord. I can think of at least five women—none of whom I like very much, I might add—who would fall at your feet and grovel to get you to their buffet tables." She looked down her nose at him in mock superiority. "Guest lists are everything, you know," she drawled, then grinned at him.

The slight smile returned to Clay's lips, albeit grudgingly. "Are you always so blunt?" he asked.

Devon met his eyes candidly. "Someone has to be. Honesty is something that doesn't exactly abound in this particular social circuit. So I suppose the answer is yes. I try to be."

Now he laughed aloud. "I'm not sure how many people at this party would agree with your approach."

Devon's expression turned curious. "Do you?"

"Agree with you? Probably more than you know."

She grinned at him again cheerfully and relaxed against the fence post. "Does that explain why I haven't seen you before?" she asked.

"In part. You're right, actually. I'm not left off many guest lists, but neither am I much of a socializer. Especially when it comes to these benefit things. People I've never heard of invite me with the chief goal of milking a few dollars out of me for some marvelous cause."

"And you think they're using you," she guessed. "Have you by any chance ever seen a shrink for this hang-up? The very idea of a benefit is to milk money out of your guests. Don't you think you're being a bit paranoid?"

Clay's shoulders grew rigid again. "I prefer to describe myself as cautious. I live by the motto that it's better to be safe than sorry."

"That could get boring." Before his wariness could claim him again completely, she pushed on blithely. "So how come you're here tonight? This is definitely a benefit. Moira's been running around with her palm out all night. You can't tell me that she hasn't gotten to you yet."

A smile broke through his control. "She's gotten to me, all right. But I genuinely like Moira and Derrick. I met them when they designed my house, and we've maintained the friendship. They're decent people." He paused suddenly, his eyes becoming speculative and shrewd. "Now that we've deciphered everything right on down to my most personal hang-ups, what about you? I haven't seen you around before either. Why? Who are you?"

Devon's smile faded abruptly. The wife of a local attorney, she answered silently, and the guilt she'd been ignoring mushroomed in her stomach again. Yet something made her choke the words back. Not now, she thought, not just yet. I'll tell him later. For the moment, she was reveling in a desperate need for the newness and novelty of their conversation, for the titillating excitement his presence sparked in her. It was an exhilarating feeling after what seemed like a lifetime of Ian's sour comments and his antisocial dependency on his brandy bottle. She forced her smile back into place.

"You probably haven't seen me around because you haven't risked enough benefits to have met me," she returned lightly. "Maybe you ought to get out and socialize more—ah!" She finished on a howl of dismay. On the other side of the fence, Southern Dance had pranced by with a frisky lack of respect for the clothing of the two people watching her. Mud spewed up from beneath her hooves and hit Devon squarely on the thigh.

"Saved by a temperamental racehorse," she muttered. She bent over to wipe unthinkingly at the mud and only managed to smear it. "Damn," she finished. "Another job for the dry cleaner."

Clay's attention to the stain on her dress was only perfunctory. His eyes came back to hers immediately. "Saved from what?" he asked.

From having to tell you who and what I am, she was going to say, but the words never got past her throat. She swallowed them deliberately and smiled up at him. "From another few hours of a hopelessly boring party, of course," she answered. "Moira would have my head if I went back to her living room covered with mud. Not to mention the fact that Derrick would know immediately where it came from. Didn't you mention that he's highly protective of his horses?"

Clay flashed her an amused grin. "Clever, aren't you?"

"I just know a good excuse for an early exit when I see one."

She had meant her words to be light, but his eyes snared hers again as she straightened up, and her answer became tight in her throat. Something in his gaze made her heart leap. She knew what he was going to say before he said it.

"I don't suppose you'd allow me to share in your good fortune?" he murmured, his eyes holding hers intently.

"I—what do you mean?" She plucked nervously at the soiled satin of her dress. It was an inane question and she knew it. Neither of them had any doubt as to what he meant.

He explained anyway, although his gaze became somewhat mocking. "If you'll let me give you a ride home, I can escape the party as well."

The expression in his eyes was just the same as it had been in the house, she thought as her pulse began to speed up again. It was calling to her, drawing her. A newfound feeling of daring exploded in her. Why not let him give her a ride home? It was no more than Derrick would have done for her, and that would have been innocent enough.

She could spend just a little more time with him. Talk to him some more. The guilt inside her screamed, but a new sense of exhilaration matched it in force. She felt light-headed with the jarring conflict of emotions, almost ill with conscience, but defiant too. It was just a ride home. And what did she have to return home to anyway? An empty house, yet another weekend alone. And then Ian would return on Monday, as morose, taciturn, and drunk as he always was after a weekend away. She bit her lip.

"I, uh . . . I came to this thing with friends," she supplied in a hushed voice.

"Is that an affirmative answer?"

It was. Oh my, yes it was. She forced a smile to her face and shrugged casually, although her heart was thundering. "Sure," she responded. "If I'm going to do something as outrageous as disappear from one of Moira's parties before nine o'clock, I might as well have an accomplice. You'll do nicely. Moira wouldn't dare get angry with you—she'll want you at her next party."

"You're making me sound more like a hostage than an accomplice," he muttered, but he was still wearing that peculiar partial smile. Devon dredged up another of her own.

"Oh, no. We're in this thing together. Now, shouldn't we have some sort of plan of action here?"

"You mean like me going in to get your coat and you slinking out to meet me at my car?" His smile became more genuinely amused.

"Exactly. I couldn't have come up with a better scheme myself."

"I thought you'd like it. It amazes me how women always manage to get the easy end of a deal."

"That," Devon answered as some of her tension eased away beneath the warm camaraderie of their conversation, "is because we're the weaker sex."

"By your own design only, I think." His response was too fast, too harsh. His smile faded abruptly as Devon stared at him in surprise. Again she got the impression that she had touched on a hang-up, but Clay didn't allow her to dwell on it. He turned away from her immediately and began striding toward the house. His walk was so confident, so self-assured, she thought.

"My car's the first white convertible you'll come to if you make an immediate left after you leave the side gate and keep walking toward the street," he called out over his shoulder, as though his tense mood of a moment before had never occurred.

What an odd man, she thought, watching him go. What an intriguing man. *Except that I'm in no position to be feeling intrigued.* She shook her head to combat the fresh surge of guilt, then began walking toward the side gate before she could change her mind.

Then, as she reached the street, she began grinning again. Clay's directions to his car had been ambiguous, but she was beginning to suspect that they had been deliberately so. There was more than one white convertible on the street, most of them Mercedes, but the first one she came to was a Rolls-Royce Corniche. It would have been so easy for so many men to have told her arrogantly, "Meet me at the white Rolls." But not Clayton Wyatt. Not this man, she thought. It occurred to her again that he almost seemed to try to hide his wealth.

The car wasn't locked, and she pulled the door open and dropped down onto the front seat. No sooner had she closed it again than Clay's voice came to her out of the shadows.

"Another caper pulled off with impeccable aplomb," he announced. He circled the car and came up to the driver's side. Pulling the door open, he tossed her fox jacket into her lap.

"Have you pulled off many in your time?" she asked, falling easily back into the cheerful banter of their conversation. She sat up and shrugged into her jacket.

Clay started the car and pulled away from the curb. "I think careful consideration would reveal that I've had more pulled on me."

Devon slanted a careful look at him out of the corner of her eye. His profile was strikingly handsome, even when he frowned as he was doing now. "You're not very trusting, are you?" she asked bluntly.

His scowl deepened. "Where am I taking you?" he responded without answering.

"Oh, I see. It's not something we want to discuss. Okay, you're taking me in the general direction of Mummy Mountain. Go west on Lincoln Drive and I'll tell you where to turn. I'm not taking you out of your way, am I? Is that a question you feel comfortable answering?"

He took his eyes off the road long enough to give her a withering look. "Is nothing sacred with you? No, I'm not incredibly trusting. Satisfied? Now can we talk about where you live?"

"I just told you. I also asked if I was taking you out of your way. If I'm going to have to feel guilty about this, I'd just as soon get it over with now."

His chuckle was deep and warm. "You don't have to feel guilty. If you live in the vicinity of Mummy Mountain, you're right on my way."

She ran her hand gently over the dashboard of the Rolls. "Why do I get the impression that we don't live in the same neighborhood?" she whispered, more to herself than to him.

"Pardon me?"

Devon shook her head. "Nothing. Take a right at the next corner." She directed him to her house, feeling some of her good humor beginning to seep away. The windows were dark, the house clearly empty. Just as it was more often than not. It seemed that Ian spent most of his time out of town. Doing what? It was a question that had been occurring to her more and more lately, but ironically, she no longer cared enough to try to answer it. Suddenly, as she glanced up at the house, she realized how horribly empty her life and her marriage were. She swallowed against the bitter despair that began to well up in her throat.

Clay brought the Rolls to a stop in her driveway and

turned to face her. His partial smile was still in place. "In the event that you're still harboring any residual guilt, you can let it go now. I live over in Tatum Canyon. You haven't taken me out of my way at all."

An ironic laugh escaped Devon. Tatum Canyon. She should have known. It was one of the most prestigious addresses in the valley. She glanced up at her house again and her smile faltered. She was sure Clay's home would be well lit and warmly inviting when he got home. It was undoubtedly a showplace. "Why do I feel like Cinderella at midnight?" she muttered aloud.

"I don't know, but feel free to leave behind a glass slipper."

His response was husky. Devon sensed an omen in it. Her breath caught in her throat and she turned back to him quickly.

He was leaning closer to her. One of his hands caught a strand of her long hair, and he wound it around his finger as he watched her intently, the speculative look back in his eyes. A shiver of panic tripped through her.

She pulled back a little until her hair slid through his fingers and fell to her shoulder again. "What are you doing?" she asked hoarsely. "Was this part of our scheme, or did I miss something?"

"You haven't missed a thing, but I have," he murmured. "What a refreshing change you are. If I had known you were doing the benefit circuit, I would have attended a lot more of them."

Devon shook her head, a nervous protest on her lips. Her guilt was beginning to tear at her. This was more than just talking, more than just a ride home. She opened her mouth to speak, but she never had the chance to respond. Clay's mouth claimed hers suddenly, effectively cutting off her words. The world around her began to whirl.

The hunger of his kisses assaulted her senses. His tongue traced the outline of her lips, then tried to explore her mouth. His lips were teasing her, daring her to respond. She tried to pull away from him, but before she had moved inches, her spine came in contact with the car door. She shuddered as a torment of emotions seethed inside her. It was all she could do not to reach out and wind her arms around his neck, welcome his touch, his embrace.

Because she wanted him. God help her, she wanted him. She wanted to scream out loud with the injustice of it all.

His thigh was hard and warm against her leg. Devon swallowed convulsively as a strange heat suffused her. Her hand fell to his thigh as though it had a will of its own; then she gasped and drew it away sharply as though he had scalded her. He had, she thought wildly. He was. The desire in his strong, hard body was palpable and it scorched her, igniting something inside her that she had never felt before.

But she had no right to feel it. Not now, not here, certainly not with Clayton Wyatt. Flirting with him was one thing and bad enough, but her conscience could never allow things to go beyond that point. She squirmed away from him emphatically and placed a trembling hand against his chest to hold him off.

"Not . . . not even a glass slipper could help in this case," she managed, her voice shaky. It occurred to her that it was probably the first honest thing she had said to him all night.

Clay leaned back and rested his elbow on the steering wheel. That same partial smile touched his lips. "Any particular reason why not? I was just beginning to think we wouldn't need it."

She shook her head and reached blindly for the door handle. She fully expected him to try to stop her and was more than a little surprised when he didn't. But then, he wasn't a very predictable man.

"No one's made a slipper to fit me yet." She blurted her response and scrambled out of the car. "Thanks for the ride and for rescuing me from the party."

"It was my pleasure." He didn't get out of the car but just sat there and continued to watch her speculatively. "A nightcap might make it even more worthwhile," he suggested after a moment. It was almost as though he had to think about it.

"Oh, God." The words came from deep in her throat and were more of a moan than anything else. She shook her head again. "I can't. I'm sorry . . . sorrier than you know," she said more audibly, then turned on her heel and hurried toward the dark house.

She had not looked back. Once inside the house, she leaned weakly against the door, guilt and remorse and disappointment churning wildly inside her. Minutes had passed while an electric silence from the driveway made her unable to move. Then finally, finally, she heard his car back out onto the street again and move away. She never saw Clay Wyatt again.

Until now. She peeked around the doorway again to find that he was still standing at the piano. How many times had she battled dark, lonely nights in the past year with memories of those shimmering green eyes, that slight half smile? How many times had she daydreamed of what might have been if she had only learned the truth about Ian's business trips three days before that benefit instead of three days after? If she had only been single then?

She squeezed her eyes shut, unaware of the fact that she was still standing in the doorway, that she hadn't backed into the shadows again. The same feelings that had churned inside her a year before came back to her full force. She swallowed convulsively.

It didn't make any difference. Not really. Those daydreams had been nothing more than wild, impossible supposition. She was divorced now, but too many other things had changed for her to be in a position to approach him. She took a deep, shaky breath and turned away from the sight of him just as she had turned away from his car a year before. She had to get out of there. She couldn't risk having him seeing her.

She was unaware of his eyes roaming idly in her direction just as she darted down the hallway. Clay stood up straight and placed his glass on the piano. Several long, sure strides took him to the doorway. For a long moment he just stood there, staring down the empty hallway.

She was gone. Had he imagined that he had seen her? Or was it someone else who just looked like her? No, that was impossible. Those wild sapphire eyes were engraved on his memory. The mystery of what had become of her had badgered him for a year. He hadn't forgotten her. He'd know her anywhere. He'd know that wealth of thick, cocoa-colored hair, that slender, reedlike frame. But more than that, he'd recognize that volatile air she had about her. He'd never forgotten that. She'd once made him think that she was just simmering, waiting for the right moment to explode. He'd once been too captivated by the contrast of hesitant vulnerability and almost haughty amusement in her eyes to forget her that easily.

He turned on his heel abruptly and searched the room. It had been Moira and Derrick Kendall's benefit he had met her at a year ago. Moira and Derrick were at this party too—somewhere. Suddenly determined, he set out to find them.

He located Moira on the patio near the pool. She glanced up at him and smiled brightly as he approached, then made a great show of looking at her watch.

"Coming to say good-night?" she teased. "It's half past nine. Isn't it getting a little late for you?"

He settled his tall frame into the chair beside her. "You'll never forgive me for sliding away so early from that benefit you gave, will you?"

Moira shrugged good-naturedly. "No way. I'm going to get as much mileage out of that as I can."

"Actually, that's what I wanted to talk to you about."

"You're finally going to apologize?" Moira prodded him, then noticed the serious look in his eyes. "No, you're not. So what is it then?"

Clay leaned forward and lowered his voice. "There was a woman at that benefit you gave."

"There were a lot of them," Moira reminded him.

"This one was here tonight too."

Moira cocked her head at him curiously. "That's not unusual."

Clay looked exasperated. "I want to know who she is," he explained.

"Okay. Point her out to me."

"I can't. She just disappeared." He paused, then added in a perplexed undertone, "Again."

Moira's eyebrows lifted. "This sounds interesting. Describe her to me."

Clay scowled. "I doubt if the things I remember about her will help you identify her." He shrugged suddenly. "She's more attractive than beautiful. In her late twenties, I'd say. Bright blue eyes. Relatively tall and thin. She's witty, cheerful. Blunt. God, I don't know."

"Outside of the last few items, you've just described half of the women here. What did she have on?"

"A blue dress that matched her eyes. She's got wavy brown hair but it was pulled back tonight, off her face, you know . . ." He trailed off, his hand motioning toward the back of his head to give her the general idea.

Suddenly, Moira laughed delightedly. "Devon Jordan," she supplied. "You've got to mean Devon."

Clay sighed and relaxed against the back of his chair. "Now we're getting somewhere. What else can you tell me about her?"

Moira grinned at him mischievously. "Nothing."

"What do you mean, nothing?"

"She's my best friend. I'm not going to sit here and gossip about her. If you want to know more about her, you'll have to ask her."

"That'll be difficult. As I just mentioned, she's disappeared."

Moira scowled. "She can't just disappear. She's—" She stopped suddenly, cutting herself off deliberately. Clay looked at her expectantly.

"She's what?" he prodded her.

"She's not in the phone book," Moira announced cheerfully, regaining her composure. "She is, however, listed in my personal address book."

"Is that supposed to do me any good?"

"Sure. But only if you call me in the morning so that I can give you her number." She settled back in her chair and watched the speculation in his eyes.

Devon didn't know it yet, but the cloistered, quiet life she'd led since her divorce was about to be shaken up. Moira smiled to herself. It was, she thought, an occurrence that was long overdue.

2

Devon would have emphatically disagreed with Moira's assessment of her life, most especially at eleven o'clock the next morning. Quiet? The phone hadn't stopped ringing all morning, although the calls hadn't had anything to do with the social whirl she had enjoyed the year before while she was still married. These calls were mostly from creditors. And cloistered? Her tiny, three-room apartment was anything but secluded and peaceful.

She leaned back in her chair at the kitchen table and ran a nervous hand over her eyes as she glanced around her apartment. Cookbooks were stacked everywhere around the kitchen. The blue dress she had worn the night before was still draped over the back of the sofa in the living room, exactly where she had left it an hour earlier. She had carried it halfway to the door, intending to take it to the dry cleaner's, before she decided that the six dollars the little Frenchman would charge her could be better put to other uses and that she could get one more wear out of the dress.

The front door was wide open, allowing the lukewarm January breeze to cool the three small rooms so that she wouldn't have to turn on the air conditioner. The money she would have to pay the electric company the next month for such a luxury could be put to other uses too. Unfortunately, cool air wasn't all that the opened door allowed in. The sounds of traffic from the street below her apartment echoed through the kitchen as she tried to concentrate on the stack of bills on the table in front of her. The neighborhood wasn't the best either. Along with the sounds of traffic came irate Mexican shouts and Anglo bellowing. She was sure that the argument was taking place right outside her door.

She had long since given up bemoaning any of it. She sighed stoically and tried to block out the noise as she braced her elbows on the kitchen table again. She leaned over to look at the invoices in front of her, but didn't really see them. Sure, she thought, the kitchen in her house near Mummy Mountain would have been much more conducive to the operation of her catering firm. This cramped apartment on the periphery of south Phoenix was hardly ideal for living in, much less for running a business out of. But Ian's philandering and gambling debts had seen to the profits from sale of the house. It had taken him six years, but he had run through every dime her parents left her, putting herself and Ian so severely in debt that everything they owned had to be sold to pay their creditors. Devon was sure that his mistress had kept her gifts and trinkets, but for her part, Devon had been left with barely enough money to pay the rent for this apartment, modest though it was.

She grimaced, trying not to think about it. If she dwelled on the injustice of it all, she would go mad. It was just the way things were, and she reminded herself that there wasn't much she could do about any of it—except pull herself up by the shoestrings the only way she knew how. She was practical. She wouldn't cry over spilled milk. She'd just clean it up.

That meant running her small catering business out of

her own kitchen, and it also meant covering the bills in front of her so that she could keep on running it. She riffled through the invoices, scowling. The two women who worked for her part-time would be willing to wait a few days for their paychecks—or at least until the check from the party she was catering that night cleared—but she hated asking them to do that again. What she needed right now was something along the lines of manna from heaven, she decided. It could come in the form of a small business loan, or it could come by way of just one really big job, but one thing was for sure—it *had* to come in some way, shape, or form if she were going to keep her head above water.

If only the people she had once socialized with didn't feel so damned awkward about using her services, she thought for the thousandth time. The crowd she had moved with during her marriage was a wealthy one. They used caterers the way most people used electricity. But the fact was that they were embarrassed and too snobbish to hire her. The Myers' party the night before had marked the first time in a year that her one-time "friends" had paid her to cater an affair rather than invite her as a guest. For that matter, they didn't invite her personally anymore either, she thought with a wry smile. Without her diamond choker, without her wardrobe and her furs, she had nothing of any social value to offer people like them. They had never appreciated her candid honesty. She was beginning to understand that she had been on their guest lists solely because of the money people hadn't known Ian was squandering.

The Myers' cocktail party the night before had been a real eye-opener in more ways than one, she thought dismally. Other than Moira and Derrick and the Myers themselves, no one had even spoken to her. Most of the guests had pretended that they didn't remember her, which was fine with Devon. Her worst fear had been that someone would mention the mess she had made of her life, that someone would rub her nose in the unfathomable naiveté she had displayed while she had been married to Ian. She had squared her shoulders and avoided their eyes, tackling the situation as best she could. She had had to. She needed the money desperately. It was no time for pride. The attitudes of her fair-weather friends, the fact that she was catering the party rather than having been invited to it, were things she had tried not to think about.

Until she had spotted Clay Wyatt standing by the piano.

She squeezed her eyes shut against the memory and leaned back in her chair again. Right after she had fled from the sight of him, she had turned the entire operation over to Gayle and Lisa, the two women who helped her out on a part-time basis. And then she had left the party. Just like that. So much for her sense of responsibility. So much for her desperate need to have the Myers' party go well so that some of the guests might also consider using her services.

But seeing Clay again had shaken her badly, more than she ever would have imagined. With all the trauma she had survived in the last twelve months, who would ever have thought that the sight of a mere man could have unglued her that way? But then, Clay Wyatt had never been a mere man, not in her memory and not in her dreams. He was the first man she had felt a spark of interest in since she had met Ian at nineteen. And with Ian, it had been a matter of shattered dependency; a police officer had shown up on her doorstep one afternoon to tell her that her parents were dead, and then Ian had magically appeared to help her pick up the pieces. In retrospect, she had to admit that her feelings for him had been nothing like the feelings Clay Wyatt ignited in her, nothing like the white-hot awareness he made her feel. She'd never felt like that before in all of her twenty-seven years.

And she had ended up running from it. But then, she hadn't had any choice in the matter, not really. What else could she have done? A vivid mental image brought a bittersweet smile to her patrician features. She could just see herself walking over to that piano and saying to him, "Hi! Remember me? You met me last year when I was an invited guest at the Kendalls' benefit. Tonight I'm the caterer."

Her smile faltered. That scenario might have been plausible, but what would have followed would have been impossible. Tell him that the change had occurred because she had been a married woman the year before when she led him on? Never. Tell him that she had been so naïve and sheltered that she hadn't had an inkling of her ex-husband's six-year affair or his misappropriations of her money? No way. That was something she detested having people know about. Having someone like Clay Wyatt know was unthinkable.

She shuddered slightly at the very thought of such mortification and bent back over the check she was writing out. She had done the only thing she could have when she left the Myers' party the night before. She hadn't dared make contact with Clay Wyatt again. And her pride wouldn't let her risk having him make contact with her.

She tore the check out of the checkbook and ran a hand through her thick, wavy hair. It was time to stop dwelling on Clay Wyatt and get back to the problems at hand. Like how she was going to cover this check at the bank before the post office delivered it to its destination. Last night was history; tomorrow needed her help.

She bit her lip and reached for the little green book that held her schedule of upcoming parties. Just as her fingers closed around it, the telephone rang. Devon groaned. Slowly, wearily, she withdrew her hand. Another creditor, no doubt. It was the first of the month. A hundred businesses were going through their past-due files, and her name was jumping out at them. Sighing, she twisted around in her chair and reached for the wall phone behind her.

"This is Devon Jordan," she answered in a mechanical voice that she hoped would sound like a telephone answering machine. She couldn't deal with another problem that day. "I can't come to the telephone at the moment, but if you'll leave your name and number at the sound of the—" She broke off suddenly, feeling a traitorous sneeze tickling her nostrils. Would nothing go right that day? Frustration hit her hard and abruptly. She covered the mouthpiece irritably and sneezed, then jumped to her feet and stalked to the open door.

"Will you two shut up down there?" she screamed to the anonymous people who were still arguing on the street below her. Turning back into the apartment, she lifted her hand from the receiver and put it to her ear.

"Hello?" she forced herself to answer brightly. She was more perturbed by the intrusion of the call than she was by the fact that the caller would undoubtedly think she was off her rocker. "This is Devon," she continued. "Can I help you?"

"Only if you'll tell me where you've been hiding for the last year," was the response of the amused male voice on the other end of the line.

Devon's heart lurched. She sat down weakly on the kitchen chair again, feeling as though her knees were about to buckle beneath her.

Clay Wyatt. So he had indeed seen her at the party the night before.

She knew beyond any doubt that it was him. She'd know his voice anywhere. She remembered so clearly the way it had floated to her on the night air a year earlier. Nervous tension mingled with a wild excitement in the pit of her stomach, making her feel almost ill. She couldn't answer him.

Clay finally took it upon himself to break the silence that was beginning to weigh down the telephone line. "When you told me a year ago that you wanted to play Cinderella, you weren't kidding," he teased. If she closed her eyes, she knew she would be able to see that peculiar partial smile on his lips. She hadn't forgotten that either.

She cleared her throat. "When I do something, I like to

33

do it all the way," she answered. "No half-way measures." Her voice sounded thin and high-pitched with nerves, even to her own ears.

"Well, you certainly did it this time." His words were followed by the soft, sultry chuckle she remembered so well. "You seem to be one of a kind, Devon Jordan. I've had women try to seduce me, I've had women propose to me, I've even had one throw her plate at me in a crowded restaurant, but no one's ever disappeared into thin air on me before."

"Don't take it to heart," she advised. Her voice seemed to grow gradually warmer and stronger. The shock of hearing from him ebbed gently out of her system. "Price Charming at least had that glass slipper we talked about," she reminded him. "I didn't leave you much to work with, if I remember correctly."

"That," he answered, "is a gross understatement."

"You found me again," she pointed out. A smile pulled at her lips. The easy camaraderie of their conversation was doing just what it had done to her a year before. It was warming a spot inside her that seemed to have been icy for a lifetime.

"Only because Lady Luck was on my side," he responded. "You covered your tracks like a con man who's just bilked a town full of people out of their entire life savings."

"I moved," she protested. "It's done all the time."

"Not the way you did it. I went back to your house a few days after I dropped you off there. It was empty, with a For Sale sign out front. You didn't even leave me your name, much less a forwarding address."

"I didn't?" she asked inanely. Her breath suddenly felt short and shallow in her throat. It was the perfect opportunity to explain to him what had happened . . . but she couldn't bring herself to do it.

"No," he responded. There was a trace of annoyance in his tone now, as though he thought she were playing games with him. "You didn't."

"It must have slipped my mind." She had to force her

voice to sound light. "How *did* you manage to get my name and number, by the way?"

"Your best friend gave it to me."

Devon's heart jumped into her throat and she coughed over it. What else had Moira told him? "Some gentleman you are," she finally managed to answer. "Your sense of honor must be a little less than impeccable."

She could see him raising his eyebrows in that way he had. "I'm almost afraid to ask, but what led you to that conclusion?" he inquired.

"Dragging information about someone out of her best friend isn't very honorable."

Clay chuckled again. "Maybe not. But it was justifiable."

"How so?"

"You brought my lack of honor upon yourself by disappearing on me twice."

"Twice?" Devon echoed, curiosity welling up inside her.

"Last year and last night," he answered. "Now what full-blooded American male is going to take that lying down? You couldn't have done a better job of arousing my curiosity if you'd tried."

"Are you giving me that look?" she asked abruptly, scowling down at the phone in her hand.

Clay sounded genuinely surprised. "What look?"

"That look you get when I tell you something and you're not sure you want to believe me. You raise your eyebrows. You did it when I first met you and told you I didn't know who you were. I'd bet money that you're doing it again now."

A full, robust laugh replaced his chuckle. "Meaning that you think I'm wondering if you deliberately disappeared to arouse my curiosity and nab my interest?"

"Bingo."

"Well, you nabbed my interest, all right. But I have trouble believing that you did it on purpose."

"Because you trust me?" she prodded him, knowing what his answer would be.

There was a short silence before he gave it to her. "No. Because if it had been a ploy, you wouldn't have waited a year to pop up again. Women don't have that kind of patience."

"I can see that you haven't made any great headway on your hang-ups since I last saw you." She had meant her words to be light, but her feminine pride was wounded. She had expected nothing more from him, yet his response still hurt. Which was ridiculous, she told herself harshly. She barely even knew the man and would probably never speak to him again anyway. She wouldn't dare.

"Anyway, just for the record, Moira volunteered your name and telephone number," he answered, changing the subject as she could have guessed he would.

Devon felt a ripple of alarm dance down her spine. "What else did she volunteer?" she asked. She was almost afraid to know.

"Absolutely nothing." She felt relief shimmer through her before he continued. "She gave me your number, but anything beyond that was like pulling teeth."

"What else is there?" she countered lightly, regaining her composure. "Would you like my social security number?"

"Even that combined with your name and telephone number leaves a lot of gaps," he answered, then paused. "Why don't you have dinner with me tonight and fill them in?"

Fill them in? Oh, God. Her heart constricted and dropped into her stomach with a thud. No, hers were gaps that were better left empty. Her pride couldn't stand seeing them filled in.

She had to turn him down. Oddly, an overwhelming disappointment threatened to swallow her. Her voice was uncharacteristically tight when she answered him. "Can't," she replied quickly. "I'm busy tonight."

"Get rid of him early. We'll have a late supper."

So he could be as determined as he was intriguing. Devon ran a shaky hand over her eyes. She was suddenly immensely grateful that she had a party to cater that night. It would be so easy to agree to see him.

"I can't do that," she managed. "I have no idea what time I'll be free to leave this . . . engagement." It was true. The party that night was a small one. Neither Gayle nor Lisa would be there to allow her to leave early. She'd have to stay until the bitter end. And bitter it probably would be, she thought, if she spent the entire night dwelling on Clay Wyatt and imagining what might have happened if she could have gone out with him.

"As I remember it," Clay answered confidently, "you're very talented at slipping away from parties early."

Tell him that you're not invited to this one. Tell him that you're catering it. Her conscience screamed at her, but she bit her lip. "Sometimes circumstances preclude my talents," she responded instead.

There was a short silence on the telephone line. She was beginning to know him well enough to suspect that he wouldn't give up. He was a cautious man, but once he made up his mind that he wanted something, he would go after it.

He didn't disappoint her. "Okay," he answered finally. "I've waited a year. I can wait until tomorrow night." His voice was both piqued and amused.

"I—" she began, knowing that she had to refuse him but not knowing how to go about it. Or was it simply that she didn't want to?

He didn't allow her time to find her voice and finish. "I'll pick you up at seven-thirty. What's your new address?"

"Forty thirty-seven East—" she began, then broke off again. Panic and a wild exhilaration danced through her. She was going to do it. She was going to have dinner with him. It had been so long, so very long, since she had had a date. Couldn't she just have dinner with him without telling him what she had been doing at the party the night before and opening up that whole can of worms?

Of course she could. And she was going to. Excitement

37

flashed through her, then died abruptly under the assault of logic. She could have dinner with him, but she couldn't allow him to see where she lived now. Her apartment was so far removed from the house she had once lived in. If he picked her up at the apartment, if he saw it, she would have a lot of explaining to do. And explaining was something she didn't want any part of the following night.

"No wait," she interjected suddenly. "I've got plans tomorrow night too."

There was a short silence as Clay seemed to weigh this. "I should warn you," he responded eventually, "that I'm not a patient man. I want to see you, Devon. I'd like to sit down and talk to you under more relaxed circumstances than those we've shared. But I'm not going to wait until next Christmas to do it."

She knew he meant it. She understood suddenly that if she turned him down, he would easily find someone else to share dinner with. The realization hurt, but it also aroused a feminine sense of competition inside her.

"I was going to suggest meeting you somewhere," she answered quietly. "And a little later than seven-thirty. Maybe eight?" The whole thing was a charade, but she had no choice but to play it out, she thought. She had no plans for the following night, but neither did she have the house near Mummy Mountain any longer.

"How about my place?" Clay suggested eventually.

"Your house?" Devon's throat closed in sudden tititlated panic. Did she dare?

"Actually, I was thinking more along the lines of the restaurant at my hotel. I find I get the best service there."

"Ah." She wasn't sure if she was disappointed or relieved. "Your place then," she went on, not wanting to think about it. "Shall we meet in the lobby at about eight?" She managed to finish with some vestige of her old brightness.

"Not the lobby. The lounge." There was a short pause before he added, "I trust you'll remember what I look like?"

She wasn't sure if he was teasing her or not. There was an edge of something serious in his voice. "Why shouldn't I?" she asked carefully.

"Because you either didn't recognize me last night or you chose not to come over and say hello."

It wasn't a matter she dared to clear up for him. Devon bit her lip. "I remember what you look like," she answered. How could she ever forget?

3

$\sim$⬥⬥⬥⬥⬥⬥⬥⬥⬥$\sim$

She was out of her mind. She *knew* she was out of her mind. But didn't they say that if you thought you were crazy, then you probably weren't?

Devon felt like a fool—on many counts—as she turned her blue Volkswagon Rabbit into the sweeping oval drive of the Wyatt Hacienda. She had no business being there. Her car looked woebegone and ridiculous in comparison with the luxury automobiles that lined the parking lot. A sign advertised valet parking, but she knew she couldn't take the management up on their offer. She didn't want to spend the extra couple of dollars that tipping would involve.

She drove the Rabbit around to the back of the parking lot, turned the engine off, and leaned forward to rest her forehead against the steering wheel. If she had any ounce of sanity left, she would turn right around and go home. Pronto. She didn't belong here.

But sanity was something she had been incredibly short on since Clay had called the day before. A small, sensible part of her mocked her heart for believing that she had anything at all to gain from one stolen night with Clay Wyatt . . . but here she was. Despite the fact that she knew that one stolen night was all it could ever be, she was keeping their date.

She had wrestled with her conscience for more than twenty-four hours. She knew she had to tell Clay she was married when she first met him and had led him on. He'd probably think that she had been doing little more than teasing him that night a year ago and wouldn't want to see her again. But she couldn't accept his hospitality for the evening and do anything else.

Of course, she knew that if she told him she'd been married, the truth about Ian would also come out. Her throat closed against the mortification of such a revelation, but there didn't seem to be any way around it. She could have broken their date, but the excitement of seeing Clay again overcame all her better judgment. She hadn't been able to find the willpower to call him and cancel.

The door of the Rabbit creaked embarrassingly as she pushed it open. It seemed to mock her very presence there at the elaborate hotel. She slammed it closed again and strode purposefully toward the ornate double doors.

Appreciative glances followed her as she made her way into the lobby, but Devon didn't notice them. If she had, she wouldn't have felt deserving of them. She felt like a fraud. She stopped in front of the planters that lined the lounge area and ran a nervous hand down her thigh to smooth the loose white knit of her dress. Swallowing against a sudden dryness in her throat, she entered the lounge.

She spotted Clay instantly. It was as though he possessed some sort of magnetism that drew her eyes to him. He sat at the bar, his back straight as he moved his glass around in idle little circles. He must have caught sight of her out of the corner of his eye, because she had taken barely three steps before he rose from his bar stool. He moved with an air of authority and an indifference to the crowd around him. She'd almost forgotten he could look like that, but she knew that if she lived to be a hundred, she'd never forget the strange partial smile that was his trademark. He trained it on her now.

She forced her legs to move again so that she could meet him halfway as he came toward her. His hand fell casually to the small of her back as he guided her to a table in a darkened corner and nodded to one of the waitresses to bring his drink. Heat seemed to radiate up her spine from their point of contact. For a second, the moment he had kissed her a year earlier was as clear in her mind as though it had happened the day before.

"I was just beginning to wonder if you were going to show up," he murmured as he helped her into a chair.

Devon raised her sapphire eyes to his in a look of amusement and held them as he sat down across from her. "I'm only ten minutes late. You shouldn't be so suspicious."

Clay leaned back in his chair to watch her with that speculative look she had never forgotten. "With you, ten minutes is cause for alarm," he answered eventually. "With anyone who can disappear the way you can, nothing should be taken for granted."

"That's encouraging."

"Is it?"

"Sure. Women don't like to be taken for granted. Maybe that's why we're generally a little bit late."

His eyes held hers intently. "And why some of you have a knack for vanishing?" he asked pointedly.

Devon opened her mouth to answer just as she caught sight of the waitress approaching their table. She nodded toward her obliquely and then offered Clay a noncommittal shrug in response to his question. Brief annoyance flashed over his handsome features before he turned to look up at the waitress.

The glass she deposited in front of him was nearly empty. "I'll have another," he told her, then turned back to Devon. "And you?"

"Bourbon and water."

When the waitress had disappeared, Clay fixed Devon

with another of his assessing glances. "Isn't that a hefty drink for a lady?" he asked.

Devon raised her eyebrows at him. "I guess that depends on your definition of a lady. If you're looking for sighing and swooning, you'll have to—" She broke off suddenly. A statuesque brunette was gliding toward their table.

"I'll have to what?" Clay prodded her before he noticed the other woman. Another look of annoyance, more pronounced this time, shadowed his eyes for a brief instant. "Donna," he greeted her flatly.

"Clay . . . how good to see you again. I was wondering what had become of you. I haven't heard from you in so long." The woman cast a cautious, insolent look at Devon and then focused her entire attention on Clay again.

Clay slowly got to his feet. It was clear from his expression that he did so grudgingly. He didn't answer the brunette. Instead, he looked down at Devon. "Devon, this is Donna Martin. Donna, Devon Jordan."

"How interesting to meet you," Devon purred, holding her hand out to the other woman. She found it impossible to keep the amusement out of her voice. The expression on Donna's face was murderous. Clay looked only slightly less displeased.

The other woman ignored her hand and Devon shrugged, dropping it back into her lap. Clay sat down again decisively.

"I'll be in town all week, if you'd like to call," Donna went on, turning slightly to upstage Devon.

"We'll see," Clay responded ambiguously.

When she had gone, he turned back to Devon. A glassy look of anger seemed to make his green eyes brighter. "You were saying?" he prompted her, clearly eager to put the intrusion of Donna behind them.

Devon grinned at him impishly. "I've forgotten now." She nodded toward Donna again, who had returned to another table. "Is that typical of my competition?" she asked.

Clay scowled. "I doubt you've got any competition. As I've said, you seem to be one of a kind." He paused, his eyebrows lifting again. "That didn't bother you?" he asked.

"Donna's visit?" Devon shrugged. "That would be a little unrealistic, wouldn't it?"

"Are you trying to tell me that you're exceedingly practical in addition to being blunt?"

Devon's expression turned thoughtful. "Exceedingly practical? I don't know. If my heart were involved, I suppose my claws would be out. I know they would be. I think if I were in love, I would tend to be possessive. But I barely know you yet, and as far as I know, there are no monasteries in Phoenix, so—" She broke off again. Now a pert blond was heading toward them. She had eyes only for Clay. Devon grinned, but this time the reflex was more forced and pained.

"I think your wild love life is catching up with you," she commented. "I thought you told me that you didn't socialize much?"

"My love life?" he echoed, looking amazed. Then he, too, caught sight of the blond. This time he rose to his feet with swift, agile grace. Before Devon could open her mouth to respond, he had caught the blond by the elbow and begun steering her in the opposite direction.

Devon, a small frown furrowing her forehead, watched him seat her at another table. The cool acceptance she had displayed notwithstanding, something tightened in the pit of her stomach. Fool, she berated herself. What she had told him was true. She barely knew him. So what if he obviously got around a bit? She'd never see him again after that night, not after she told him . . .

Her thoughts trailed off as Clay returned to their table. She smiled past the lump of fledgling jealousy in her throat. "Is this going to go on all night?" she asked, her voice sounding sarcastic despite the fact that she hadn't meant it to. "I might be practical, but I'm short on patience. I thought the purpose of tonight was to talk under more relaxed circumstances."

His eyes were cold as they met hers again. His annoyance was so complete that she couldn't be sure if he was angry with her or with the other women, although she suspected that it had something to do with women in general. She seemed to remember him having difficulty in that area too, in addition to the one regarding trust.

"No, this is *not* going to go on all night," he answered shortly. "As a matter of fact, if it's okay with you, I'd like to suggest that we go upstairs to the penthouse now."

"The penthouse?"

His gaze became almost mocking. "Commonly located on the top floor," he explained. "We can have our dinner served there and enjoy a little bit of privacy."

"You invited me to dinner in your restaurant," she pointed out. Her smile was as slight and as reserved as his. "You know, this sounds an awful lot like the old I've-run-out-of-gas routine. You wouldn't by any chance be planning to seduce me, would you?"

"I can assure you that that's not my intention," he answered dryly.

Devon met his eyes as her smile widened. "Thanks loads," she drawled, getting to her feet.

Clay gave her a withering look. She had hoped to lighten his mood, but it obviously hadn't worked. Little spots of color touched his cheekbones. Yes, he was clearly upset, she thought. Just because a couple of women had stopped by to say hello to him? There's more here than meets the eye, she decided.

"The point is," he explained as he led her out of the lounge, "that my reputation is hardly that of a lady-killer. Contrary to appearances, I *don't* socialize all that much. I'm generally too busy. I can assure you that you're as safe with me in a secluded penthouse as you are in a crowded restaurant." He paused as they neared the elevator, then continued in an undertone, "And I'm not sure I'm up to the circus in the restaurant tonight."

The elevator doors opened onto a rose-hued corridor lined with delicate-looking sconces. "Surely you had to know that it would happen," she answered equably as he led her into the penthouse suite, which was another study in rose and fragile-looking silver.

At his uncomprehending look, she explained, "Your circus," and settled herself on the sofa.

Clay cast a dark look over his shoulder at her as he picked up the telephone. He spoke to someone about having their dinner served upstairs, then returned to the sofa. As he sank down beside her, Devon caught a faint whiff of his aftershave. Subtle yet distinct, she thought, so like the man himself. Her pulse quickened as she realized how badly she wanted to get to know Clay Wyatt . . . then limped nearly to a stop as she understood again that she probably wouldn't have the chance.

She studied the shimmering, magnetic green of his eyes unconsciously as he leaned back against the cushions. "They should deliver a bottle of wine in a few minutes," he murmured by way of explanation for his phone call. "And they'll bring dinner up in an hour or so. You *do* like lamb? It's a specialty of the kitchen. I took the liberty . . ." He trailed off suddenly as he became aware of the way she was watching him. His peculiar smile touched his lips again. "The hell with my liberty, right? You're waiting for me to answer your question. And if I don't, you'll ask me again and again . . . and again. It's one of the things I remembered most about you. Your propensity for being direct, not wasting words or sparing feelings. Foolish feelings, at least."

The sooty lashes that shadowed Devon's cheeks flew up in surprise. "My question?" she repeated, focusing in on his words again.

"About whether or not I knew that those little scenes downstairs would occur."

"Did you?"

He sighed thoughtfully just as a muted, careful knock sounded at the door. She felt reasonably sure that he would use the interruption to change the subject, but he surprised her by picking up where he left off after the steward had dropped off the wine. "I suspected," he responded tightly, leaning over the cocktail table to fill their glasses. "I'm also naïve enough to hope—time and time again—that it won't happen. That each successive night will be different from the last. I ought to know better by now." He paused, handing her her glass. "Women amaze me," he finished.

Devon felt her muscles tighten fractionally. So she had been right. He did have a shadowy, undefined problem regarding women. His sore spots went deeper than just trust and money.

"How so?" she asked, her voice careful.

"They tend to be an amazingly shallow and superficial breed," he answered abruptly. "I can well imagine how those scenes downstairs appeared to you. But the truth of the matter is that I dated both of those women—once. Just once. When they look at me, they don't see a man. They see dollar signs. I refuse to put up with that." His voice was vehement.

"Ah, the old identity, I'm-being-used, hang-up. It all ties in." She took a sip of her wine as she held his gaze over the rim of her glass. "You still haven't seen anyone for that?"

Clay scowled. "I told you before—I prefer to live cautiously instead."

"And I told you before that that sounded boring." She had intended her voice to be blithe and light. Instead, it came out nearly strangled. She sat up straight and deposited her glass on the cocktail table with a nervous little click. Her thoughts were whirling. There was so much going on inside this man, so much that she wanted to understand. But it was becoming more and more clear that if she told him the truth about their initial meeting, she would never see him again. Just how cautiously did he live? How would he react if he knew that—seemingly, at least—she had more reason than most to want him for his money? How would he feel if he knew that the woman dripping diamonds he had met the year before was spending her time juggling creditors?

Clay reached for her wineglass. "More?" he asked.

Devon cleared her throat carefully. "Sure," she answered. She accepted the glass from him, then blurted, "You're generalizing, you know. Horribly."

"About women?" He looked up at her again as though seeing her for the first time. He had the good grace to look slightly embarrassed. "That wasn't highly tactful of me, was it? I certainly didn't mean to imply that you had anything in common with Donna or the other woman who approached me down in the lounge."

Tell me that after you know the truth, she thought, but she bit down on her lip to keep the words inside. "Why?" she asked instead. "Why are you so suspicious? That kind of a reaction usually comes from feeling bitter about something."

The look he gave her was guarded. "Usually," he agreed.

"Are you? Bitter about something, that is?"

He chuckled suddenly. "I should have known you wouldn't let it drop."

Devon smiled at him cheerfully. "Well, I'm curious. If I don't ask, I'll never know."

He shrugged, but it seemed to her that the gesture was forced. "I suppose I might still be bitter about my marriage, although I've never really thought about it. That all happened so long ago."

"What happened?"

He gave her a withering look. "I suppose you want this from the beginning."

"It's generally a good place to start."

He refilled their glasses again and settled back against the sofa. For a moment, she doubted that he would answer her. Then he began speaking, his voice a dull monotone. "I met Gina when I was eight years old. Her family moved into our neighborhood, into a tenement down the street that was a carbon copy of ours."

"A tenement?" She slid her shoe off and curled her leg beneath her, unconsciously leaning closer to him as interest quickened inside her. "You were poor?"

"That's putting it mildly. I doubt you could imagine if I told you about it."

Oh, you don't know, she thought, but again she bit her lip against the words. "Try me," she said instead.

"No." His response was flat and abrupt. "Suffice it to say that both Gina and I came from poor families. We each had one thing going for us. I had ambition. Gina had her looks. From the time I first met her, she had every kid on the block trailing after her with his heart on his sleeve."

"And you were no exception?" Devon guessed.

"To coin your phrase, bingo." The word sounded incongruous coming from his lips. Even he seemed to realize it, and he smiled slightly before he went on. "Anyway, I was the one to win her heart. I married her when I was nineteen. To give her credit, she suffered right along with me in the early days. I worked in my father's butcher shop. Then he died and things began to change."

"How so?"

"He left me the butcher shop and I turned it into a grocery store. Money started coming in—at least in bigger quantities than it had before."

Devon nodded thoughtfully. "And money was the root of all your evils," she speculated, remembering the way he had downplayed his wealth.

He cocked an eyebrow at her. "You could put it that way," he answered. Before he could go on, another soft knock sounded at the door and their dinner was wheeled in. Clay looked up at the waiter blankly, as though he had forgotten ordering and couldn't imagine what the man was up to. His thoughts were, she realized, in a completely different time and place. She understood suddenly that he didn't tell this story often.

When they were seated at the table over the mouth-watering aroma of the lamb, she prodded him. "You were telling me about your ex-wife," she reminded him. "And about your hang-up regarding money."

She sensed more than saw his hard, agile body stiffen

in surprise. "I don't remember saying that I had a hang-up about money."

"You didn't have to."

He gave her one of his long, assessing looks. "I was right. You really don't pull any punches, do you?"

"Life's easier when you don't," she responded flatly, remembering all the times during her marriage that she had kept her head buried in the sand.

Clay cut into his lamb. He chewed thoughtfully for a minute before he deliberately changed the subject back to their original conversation. "I sold the grocery store to buy a motel," he told her. "Then I sold that to buy a hotel. Eventually I started building the chain I've got now. It was a long, uphill climb. Gina stuck it out until the bitter end."

Devon frowned at him. "Well, that's good, isn't it? That she stuck by you through it all?"

Clay's partial smile claimed his lips again. It was incredibly cynical now. "She didn't stick by me," he answered. "She stuck by my potential. That's different. After I finally made it, she left me for someone else. He was as painfully broke as I was when she married me. But not for long. Gina used my money to buy them a home. I didn't intentionally keep tabs on her, but she managed to do it all right under my nose. We'd long since moved out of the tenement area into one of the finest suburbs of Chicago. The house she bought was right down the street from the one we lived in. It was furnished with our furniture. Our Mercedes was sitting in the garage. She'd taken it all when she walked out on me, up to and including our savings account. I came home one day to find her gone, and that was all she wrote. Literally," he added in a facetious voice.

Devon grimaced, searching for something comforting to say. The faint lines around his mouth were etched deeply now with tension, and she found herself wanting to ease it. Her fingers itched to reach out and soothe the lines away.

"Well," she ventured softly, "it might have been

worse. I get the impression that she didn't hit you for a huge divorce settlement."

Clay shook his head. "No, she just left. The divorce was relatively amicable. I let her have all the things she had taken and she allowed the divorce to go through without a hitch. Of course, she was probably just afraid that if I wanted to get nasty about the whole thing, I could have sued her for adultery and she would have ended up walking away without a dime."

"Why didn't you sue her for adultery?"

Clay's expression was that of a man who just wanted to forget. "I just wanted to wash my hands of her, I suppose. I was hurt. I wanted to put it all behind me as quickly as possible."

Devon nodded. That much she could sympathize with. She knew all about putting a marriage behind you at any cost, even a great financial one.

"Well, at least you didn't have to pay her alimony," she said, trying again.

"I almost wish I had. I'm not sure that I wouldn't have felt better if the whole thing had been decided by a disinterested third party, such as a judge. I think what got to me most of all was the way she did it—that, and the fact that she felt compelled to leave a note to explain her actions. She couldn't just leave and sue me for incompatibility or some such innocuous thing, then let a judge divide things up. She had to run off and leave me with the knowledge that she had never really loved me, that she had married me because I had the most promise of any guy in the old neighborhood. She took a gamble and it paid off. I struck it rich. That was all she had been waiting for."

His voice was smooth, even nonchalant, as he finished. His demeanor was as polished as though they had been discussing the weather. Only his right hand and the slightly hard curve of his lips betrayed his agitation. His fingers tightened almost dangerously around his wine glass. His knuckles looked faintly white in the dim light.

Devon noticed all of it. His tension plucked at her own

51

nerves, mingling with a panic all her own that was rapidly beginning to take her over. She swallowed hard against a piece of lamb that was trying to stick in her throat.

He wasn't over Gina. Like little waves created by a pebble thrown into a pond, Clay Wyatt was still suffering reverberations from his experience with his ex-wife and a trust that had been misplaced. Devon suddenly knew she couldn't tell him about the current circumstances of her life—not now, not knowing what she did about him. The situation suddenly meant much more than just clearing the slate for the sake of her conscience. Now his ego was at stake.

She knew, just as well as she knew her own name, that he would think she was after him just for his money if he guessed the truth. She couldn't tell him. She couldn't do that to him. He would suffer other blows to his ego simply by virtue of his financial position, but none of them were going to be by her hand.

She swallowed again, more convulsively this time, and pushed her plate away. She had to get out of there. This stolen night was not at all what she had thought it would be.

"I've got an early appointment tomorrow," she began. "I—"

"Oh, no, you don't. Not again."

She glanced up at him quickly, startled. "I don't what?"

"Every conversation we've had has centered around me. What about you? Have you ever been married? You might as well talk. I'm not going to let you disappear again until you've told me something about yourself." His smile was teasing, but she sensed a seriousness behind it. Her heart did a nose dive into her stomach.

An hour earlier she would have forced herself to use the opening and tell him the truth. She would have told him about Ian, about how he had been her husband that night the year before, about how he had left her penniless. Now she couldn't bring herself to open her mouth. She stared at him, her eyes stricken.

"I . . . ah . . ." She paused to collect herself, then forced a bright smile to her lips. "There's not much to tell. I never had a childhood sweetheart to fall in love with," she told him honestly enough. "I went to a private school for girls and never dated much. As life stories go, it's pretty boring."

Clay's eyes became speculative again. "That's not much of an answer. It doesn't tell me if you were ever married or not."

Devon managed to maintain an enigmatic smile, although her heartbeat quickened. "Perhaps it wasn't meant to be an answer," she responded.

"No? Why not?" His partial smile became amused.

"Mystery is half the secret of a woman's appeal, isn't it?" she countered.

He chuckled softly again. The sound seemed to warm the air. She was coming to love the sound of his laugh . . . even though she was hardly in a position to afford to.

"My first impression of you was right," he answered eventually. "You are clever. Trust me when I tell you that you're appealing enough. If mystique has anything to do with it, you're the most appealing woman in the world. Not even Moira would tell me anything about you."

"I've got my friends well trained," she answered lightly, then paused. "Actually, I've got a private streak that goes relatively deep," she finished.

"Are you trying to tell me that I've got to earn your confidence?"

She forced a grin and got to her feet. "Nothing so serious as that," she answered, knowing that she had to change the subject, and fast. "Dinner was delicious. The conversation was better."

Annoyance, shadowy and subtle, touched Clay's features. He rose to his feet as well. "Is that a clue that you're leaving?"

Devon forced herself to nod. "I have to."

"Have to? Or want to?" he asked, accurately enough to ring little bells of alarm in the back of her brain. "I get the impression that you'd rather do anything than talk about yourself."

The smile she gave him was empty of humor. She was beginning to feel trapped. "Wasn't it Voltaire who said that the secret to being tiresome is in telling everything?" she asked tightly.

He didn't return her smile. Clouds of warning were beginning to settle in his eyes. "I think it's a safe guess to say that you've never been accused of being tiresome."

"No, and I don't intend to be." She reached nervously for her purse. "Don't push me, Clay. I said I've got to go now, and I mean it."

"Before you've even finished chewing your last bite? You're not leaving. You're running."

It took everything she had to keep her voice strong and decisive. Why couldn't he just understand that it would be better for both of them if she left? She had been wrong to come here. She should have known that it would be impossible to tell him the truth.

She cleared her throat and began backing toward the door. "I'm sorry," she said in a voice that was anything but conciliatory. "I should have warned you ahead of time that I couldn't stay late."

"How could you have warned me? You didn't know until a few minutes ago that I was going to ask you about yourself."

The mockery in his voice ran deep. His expression hadn't changed at all, but she was beginning to get the impression that he was stalking her, bent on revenge. For each of her unsteady steps toward the door, he took one as well. Her pulse began to hammer. What had she gotten herself into? She took another step backward and her spine came into contact with the door. "Clay . . ." she began hesitantly.

He might not even have heard her. He continued moving toward her, closing in on her. She couldn't retreat any further. Suddenly she became aware of the heat of him. It made her feel slightly light-headed and feverish. She raised a hand to his chest to ward him off, knowing only that she had to but beginning to forget why.

"You . . . you told me that I would be perfectly safe with you up here," she reminded him breathlessly, grabbing for the first plausible excuse to deny him that came to mind.

"That was before you decided you wanted to be appealing and maintain your mystery." His voice was a sultry whisper. His fingers caught her wrist and pulled her hand away from his chest. He pushed her arm down to her side almost effortlessly and moved still closer to her. She thought she could now literally feel the magnetism of him that she had only sensed before. It was almost palpable and hot. She felt herself flushing as his hips pressed into hers and she could no longer ignore his desire.

"You did it, you know," he went on. "You played with my interest and you caught it in a big way. Now you can pay the price. I want you. I don't intend to allow you to disappear on me a third time."

He lowered his head to hers, his hard body giving her no chance to escape. She knew that he was going to kiss her, yet the touch of his lips on hers still sent ripples of shock through her. For a year she had yearned for this in her dreams. She had never dared to believe that it would happen again. Now that it was, her breath caught almost painfully in her throat in a silent gasp of awe.

He pinned her against the door as his mouth claimed hers. Devon felt the heat of him infuse her. It made her pulse thunder, her blood roar through her. She closed her eyes and felt as though she were catapulting through a time tunnel. It was as though the year since Moira's benefit had never passed. She still wanted this man with a wild, alien part of her that knew no conscience, no restrictions.

And she still couldn't have him.

She was poor. And he was rich, too rich. Because of his past wounds, he'd never be able to see past her current circumstances. There was no future in this, no hope for them. She groaned low in her throat at the injustice of it all.

Clay took the sound as one of pleasure and his kiss deepened. The touch of his lips became harder, more forceful. His mouth covered hers hungrily. When his tongue began to explore the recesses of her mouth, Devon felt her head begin to swim. The caress of his tongue against hers, so roughly provocative, virtually demanded a response from her. And she wanted to give it, desperately.

Longing lay coiled in the pit of her stomach as his free hand buried itself in the cloud of her hair. When his fingers began to trail lazily down her jaw, her breath caught again. She held it as his hand grazed her collarbone, then closed around her breast. Then her breath escaped her in a sigh. His touch was so intimate, so perfect. His fingers found her nipple through the fabric of her dress and teased it, eliciting a thunderous magic from the very core of her. She groaned shakily.

She wanted, needed, to give herself up to him, to forget the barriers between them. His touch, his kiss, were everything she remembered they were. His body was as unyielding and hard as she remembered. His thighs felt taut and rigid against her legs. His chest crushed her breasts as his hand slid to her waist and around to the small of her back and pulled her against him. She could feel herself spiraling downward into a vortex of yearning. She shuddered uncontrollably at the titillating feel of him, then swallowed convulsively.

This was impossible, hopeless.

She dredged up the last of her willpower and forced herself to turn her face away. Clay's mouth, warm and moist, slid seductively across her cheek.

"Clay . . . no," she gasped. "This can't happen."

He might have expected her withdrawal a few minutes earlier, but it seemed to take him by surprise now. His grip on her wrist weakened and he leaned away from her a bit to search her eyes. It was all the edge she needed.

She slid out from between him and the door, pulling free of his grasp.

For a long moment she stood perfectly still. Her eyes closed, she tried to catch her breath and calm the tremors of desire that rocked through her. Then she slowly opened her eyes again to meet his. They were glittering and hard as ice.

"Care to tell me why not?" he asked. His voice was a deadly purr, too controlled.

Tell him. Tell him the truth. Her conscience screamed at her, but her common sense kept the words from her lips. He wouldn't understand. He wouldn't be able to see that she had come that night simply because of a burning memory that hadn't died and a fascination with the man behind the green-crystal eyes. He would think the worst. He had been conditioned to it.

She shook her head fretfully and reached blindly for the doorknob. He didn't try to stop her when she yanked the door open, although she was almost certain he would. Then she remembered that a year before, when she had suddenly jumped out of his car, he hadn't stopped her either. His desire had been tangible then too. But there was a stronger part of this man than desire, a part that was distrustful, reticent, and cautious. She saw that in his eyes, and she understood it now.

He wouldn't try to stop her. He wouldn't risk his ego on the chance that he'd fail, and he wouldn't forget the possibility that he might be better off not getting too close to her.

Her heart thundered as she stepped out into the hall on legs so weak that she wondered if they would continue to support her. "I told you once," she answered finally, "and I'll tell you again. There's no glass slipper to fit me, Clay. This is one fairy tale without a happy ending."

For a long moment after the words fell from her lips, she just stood there. She could see the struggle for comprehension in his eyes. They were murky with puzzlement now. She longed to reach out and wipe the frown lines away, to tell him that none of it mattered. But it did matter. It mattered to him much more than it did to her, even if he didn't know it yet. She wrenched her eyes away from him and turned away.

The last thing she heard was the crack of the penthouse door slamming as she made yet another panicky escape from the lure of those unforgettable eyes.

4

~~∘∘∘∘∘∘∘∘∘∘∘~~

Two weeks later, she still couldn't get the memory of that kiss out of her mind. Neither could she forget the sound of the penthouse door slamming. It still echoed through her brain like a death knell.

She heard it now even more than she heard the sounds of traffic as she maneuvered the Rabbit through rush-hour traffic. Why? she wondered frantically. Why couldn't she just forget it? She had been kissed before. But never had she gone through this kind of turmoil.

Was it just the frustration of the whole thing? She *had* felt like Cinderella that night, stepping out of her pressure-filled world and into Clay's glamourous one, knowing that she didn't belong there anymore. She had gone into it knowing that it would be just one night, that nothing could come of it. Perhaps she would have slipped out of it all as though waking from a pleasant dream if he hadn't kissed her.

But he *had* kissed her. And she couldn't forget it.

Because she had wanted him so desperately? she

wondered. Because the ardor she had felt in him reawakened year-old yearnings, because his desire for her had been so tangibly hot and exciting? Because she had never stopped wanting him from the first time he had kissed her and she had known that she still couldn't have him?

She shook her head unconsciously. Who knew? She was sure of only two things. Clay Wyatt still wasn't over his ex-wife's betrayal; that much was as clear as a neon sign. And if he knew that she was flat broke, all of his old fears would light up like a Christmas tree.

There was no future for them. She couldn't deny that.

The car in front of her stopped suddenly for a yellow light, and Devon was forced to relinquish her thoughts. She slammed on the brakes, her heart in her throat. She shivered slightly as she realized what a close call she'd had. The bumper of the Rabbit was only inches from that of the other car. She bit her lip and swore softly. She *had* to stop dwelling on Clay Wyatt.

As the traffic started to move again, she made a deliberate effort to ease him from her thoughts. So many other things had been closing in on her lately, demanding her attention. Obviously foremost was the Rabbit with its questionable brakes. She needed to have them replaced. She didn't have the money to have them replaced. Her head swam with the pressure of it all. Twenty minutes earlier she had learned that she wouldn't have the money for quite awhile. She had appealed to her bank for a small business loan and had been turned down. Now her only hope was a really big party to cater, one that would yield a sizable check and bring in other jobs of the same magnitude. She couldn't even bear to think of the repercussions if that didn't happen.

And with all this, she was still worrying about Clayton Wyatt. She had to be out of her mind.

She scowled as she swerved into the parking lot of her apartment building and then juggled her keys restlessly as she made her way to her door. Just as she began to insert them into the variety of locks, she heard her telephone start to ring inside. Her nerves tightened as she hurriedly released the last of the locks and mentally counted the rings. She didn't dare ignore the call. There was always that slim chance that it might be a job.

She burst into the apartment and took three long strides toward the phone before she froze. What if it was Clay?

That was stupid. Expecting him to call *now* was nothing short of egotistical and wildly unrealistic. The man had a strong sense of pride. Wasn't that the root of all his hang-ups? And she had turned him down three consecutive times after that nerve-wracking night two weeks earlier. The last time had been ten days before. He hadn't called since. He wouldn't call now. It was obvious that he'd lost interest.

She forced herself to resume her dash to the phone, ignoring the pang of remorse in her stomach that came with the thought. She was *relieved* that he hadn't kept calling, she reminded herself. It offered her an easy way out of a sticky, no-win situation.

"Hello?" she gasped, collapsing back against the wall to catch her breath. She tucked the receiver between her ear and her shoulder and pressed her hand against her chest.

"Okay, I've gotten the message that you don't want to eat with me. How do you feel about skiing?"

At the sound of his voice, her throat closed. Clay. Again. He hadn't given up. Elation that she had no right to feel charged through her. It kept her throat tight. She couldn't breathe. She sank down weakly in a kitchen chair.

"I never said I didn't want to eat with you," she managed.

"You've turned down three dinner invitations in a row." Despite the fact that he obviously intended his voice to be careless, tension laced it.

"I was busy," she lied.

"Busy," he echoed sarcastically. His voice was gradually growing harder, as though he were beginning to

61

doubt his sanity for calling again. "And are you too busy to go skiing this weekend?"

Devon grimaced. She had to be busy. But did she have the willpower to turn him down a fourth time—especially knowing beyond a doubt that there would never be a fifth chance? The fact that this was her last opportunity rang in his voice, an unspoken thought but clear all the same.

She stalled for time, her thoughts whirling. "I hate to break this to you, but I don't think Phoenix is the place to ski. I've lived here almost eight years now and I've never seen a single snowflake. As a matter of fact, I don't think I've even seen the mercury dip below forty."

A short silence weighed down the telephone line. He seemed to be gauging her response, deciding if he wanted to push the issue or not. "I was thinking more along the lines of flying up to Denver," he responded eventually, carefully.

"When?" Oh, God, what was she doing? She couldn't go, didn't dare go.

But she wanted to. She wanted desperately to see him again, to be touched by him again. Her stomach constricted with the conflict between her heart and her head and she winced.

"I was planning to fly up tomorrow morning," he answered. "I've got some business to attend to at the Denver hotel. I keep a cabin nearby, so I thought I'd unwind there for a couple of days after I get things wrapped up." He paused, and she knew that he was weighing his next words meticulously. That Wyatt pride, she thought. It both fascinated and frightened her.

"I'd like you to join me," he went on eventually. There was no inflection of emotion in his voice. If she turned him down, he'd get out of it with his ego intact, and he'd tell himself that it was all for the best.

If she turned him down? She had to turn him down. "I . . . uh, I don't ski," she told him inanely. The words were disgustingly ambiguous, and she knew it. They were neither a rejection nor an acceptance.

There was another long pause before Clay answered. "I figured as much," he responded flatly.

There was a ring of finality in his voice. It broke through her control as nothing else could. "Actually, it's just that I haven't been on skis since I was sixteen," she blurted. "And even then, I wasn't very good. I grew up on the east coast, in Boston. My parents always kept a cabin in Vermont. They went up to the mountains relatively often, but I tagged along with them only once in awhile. Well, mostly I was away at school, but I guess the truth of the matter is that I didn't have the talent or the interest to go with them and learn anyway. I—" She broke off suddenly, embarrassed and horrified. She was babbling. Worse, she was reinforcing his notion that she had money. It was only another lie of omission, but it galled her. Her conscience badgered her to continue, to tell him that her parents had been fairly wealthy but that her ex-husband had taken care of the fortune they had left her, spending it on his mistress and his gambling debts, that her parents were dead and the money was gone now.

But the words stuck in her throat. She wanted to speak them, but the memory of Clay's face when he had told her about his ex-wife flashed in her mind's eye. She couldn't bring herself to open her mouth.

"Worrying about your mystery again?" Clay's taunting voice interrupted her thoughts.

"My mystery?" she echoed, wondering if she had missed part of the conversation.

"For a minute there, I thought you were actually going to tell me all about yourself."

"Don't bet your fortune on it." Her words were instinctive and quick, but they got her point across. Clay changed the subject.

"You don't have to be able to ski to go to Denver and enjoy the novelty of snow," he pointed out. "That is, of course, unless you're too busy."

His voice challenged her. That, coupled with her longing to see him again, weakened her resolve. She sighed and ran a shaky hand over her eyes. She felt like an alcoholic who needed a drink. Agreeing to see him again would be so easy . . . and so wrong. Oh, God, why had he called again? She wasn't strong enough to stay away from him.

But she had to stay away from him. If she saw him again, it would only mean embroiling herself even further in a situation based completely on lies.

Unless she came clean with him. Her eyes narrowed as the possibility picked at her brain, then she shook her head. No way. Not yet. He wouldn't be able to handle it.

Then a new thought occurred to her, one that she hadn't dared consider before. He couldn't handle it *yet*. But maybe later, if their relationship developed . . . Maybe then she would mean enough to him so that her financial situation wouldn't matter. Maybe then she could tell him the truth. Maybe.

She knew suddenly that it was a chance she was going to take.

"Are you . . . uh, flying up first thing in the morning?" she asked tentatively.

"My flight leaves Sky Harbor at eight-thirty. It's not booked. I can get you a seat." He wouldn't beg. His voice was matter-of-fact, almost cold.

"No," she answered quickly, her thoughts spinning busily. She couldn't fly up with him and risk having him pick her up at her apartment. And she wouldn't allow him to pay for her air fare. She had her pride too, and in a situation where money was such a delicate issue, she wanted to be careful. She would need time to borrow the air fare from Moira. And a coat. She'd need a coat. She grimaced as she remembered the fox jacket she had sold to meet the expenses of her first catering job. The weather in Phoenix had never warranted replacing it with something cheaper.

"You're not giving me much notice," she went on before he could take her single negative response as a refusal and hang up. She knew that he would do precisely that if he were given half a chance. "I can't possibly leave so early in the morning," she rushed on. "The best I can do is meet you up there later in the day."

"Then you'll come?" His voice was initially reserved, then grew harder. "No games, Devon. If you say you'll be there, then you damned well better show up."

She took a long, shaky breath. "I will," she promised in a whisper.

"Then call the hotel in Denver and leave a message for me when you know what time your flight will be arriving. I'll meet you at the airport." There was another short pause. "And Devon?" His voice was a velvet warning.

"Yes?"

"I mean it. Be there. I don't forgive games. At least not more than once or twice, and you've used up your quota."

The line went dead in her hand. Devon replaced the receiver shakily. What had she gotten herself into? He wasn't a man to be toyed with. What would he do if he knew she was playing the biggest game of her life with him?

Perhaps, she thought, the secret was in just not thinking about it. If she dwelled on it too much, her conscience would drive her to the nearest insane asylum. Yes, it was better just to act, to follow her heart . . . and pray that he'd come to care for her enough so that the truth could be told easily and without repercussions at a later date.

She got up from the kitchen chair again and grabbed her keys decisively. Now was as good a time as any to see Moira and beg a favor from her. A year-old, familiar warning bell sounded in the back of her brain with the thought and she grimaced. Borrowing more money was the last thing in the world she needed to do right now. It would only put her more deeply into debt. Maybe she ought to take the rest of the day and think about what she was doing.

But she had promised Clay that she would be there.

And what was another couple hundred of dollars when she was already indebted for thousands? She needed this, she rationalized. She needed to get away.

She needed to see Clay Wyatt again.

Well, what difference did it make? Air fare to Denver was cheap. So it would be a small gift to herself. Besides, Moira owed her a favor. Devon had yet to get her hands on her for giving Clay Wyatt her phone number in the first place. She squared her shoulders determinedly, pushed her misgivings to the back of her brain, and headed for the door.

"You want to *what?*" Moira looked away from the flowers she was arranging to gape at Devon over her shoulder. Devon forced herself to meet her eyes squarely as she sank down into the chair nearest the French doors, the same chair Clay had been sitting in the first time she had laid eyes on him. There was poetic justice in that somewhere, she supposed. She looked away from Moira to give great attention to smoothing the arm covers on the chair.

"Borrow about two hundred dollars," she repeated. "Can you do it?"

Moira left the flowers and crossed slowly to a nearby loveseat. "Of course I can," she answered, sinking down onto it. "That's not the part that's giving me a headache."

Devon ignored her gibe. "I figure two hundred will cover air fare and give me something to fall back on while I'm up there. I hate to ask you, but I paid Gayle and Lisa yesterday, so I'm broke until that anniversary party on Tuesday."

Moira shook her head. "I told you—the money's no problem. My concern is that you're losing your marbles. You can't do this."

"Sure I can. It's been a rough week. I haven't had a job since last Friday. The bank turned down my loan this afternoon. I'm at my wit's end. I just need time to get away and decide where I'm going to go from here."

"Like hell you do." Moira's response was brusque, her eyes shrewd. Devon was forced to look away from her. "You've gone head over heels for this guy. That's the only reason you want to go."

"Well, so what? You've been telling me for months that I need to get away," Devon muttered, inspecting her fingernails.

"Not with Clay Wyatt. And not under these circumstances."

Devon's eyes snapped back to Moira's. "You were the one who gave him my telephone number in the first place! What did you expect to happen?"

Moira shrugged guiltily. "I don't know. I suppose I just wanted to light a fire under you to get you out and dating again. You were turning into a workaholic, Devon. I had visions of you having a nervous breakdown or some such thing. I know that the last year hasn't been easy on you, and I just wanted to help. I never thought you'd get yourself in a mess like this in a million years. It was just supposed to be one little date to get you back into the swim of things again!"

"Well, I'm swimming, all right," Devon agreed wryly. "Look, Moira, calm down. I'm not stupid, after all. I know this can't go on forever. Sooner or later I'll have to tell him I'm broke, or he'll find out somewhere else. But I can cross that bridge when I come to it. In the meantime, I've just got to cover my tracks a little bit. The way to fill him in is *not* in the form of letting him see that apartment I'm renting. That would be too much of a rude awakening. My God, we'd never get past the shell shock!"

"You probably won't anyway. You're deceiving him, Devon. Dangerously." Moira shook her head and sighed. "Don't do this. It's crazy. If you have to go to Denver, fine. Call him and come clean with him first. But don't go up there under false pretenses."

"I'm not sure I have a choice," Devon muttered. "God knows I'd take it if I did."

Moira frowned at her thoughtfully. "You're probably right there," she mused, then tried again. "Listen,

Devon, why don't you just stay in town this weekend and think this thing through a little more? Get out and broaden your horizons. Clay's the first man you've dated since your divorce. Maybe you're going a little overboard on this."

"Are you trying to insinuate that I'm on the rebound? Moira, I've been divorced for a year."

"Well, okay. So you're not exactly on the rebound. But I still think you should give someone else a try." Suddenly, she snapped her fingers. "Russ Sumner!" she exclaimed.

"Russ?" Devon looked at her doubtfully. She didn't like the way her friend's thoughts were turning.

"Sure," Moira went on. "Everytime I see him, he asks about you. Why don't you stay in town this weekend and go out with him? I'd put money on the fact that he'd drop everything if he thought you were available. I could give him a call. Who knows?" she rushed on, warming to the idea. "You might date him for awhile and find out you like him."

Devon stared at her unbelievingly. "Russ is a wimp, Moira. He breaks dates to have dinner with his mother!"

"He's also very comfortable financially."

Devon sat up straighter in her chair. "What are you saying?" she asked in a hushed voice.

Moira shrugged carefully, knowing she was treading on dangerous ground. "Don't get upset. I'm just thinking that someone like Russ might be just what you need," she responded slowly. "He's a genuinely nice guy, Devon. A decent person. You can't deny that. And he would take care of you. You could give up this struggle with the catering business and stop running yourself ragged."

Devon was out of her chair in a second. She paced the room angrily for a few minutes before she trusted herself to speak. "I don't believe you!" she finally exclaimed. "Stop playing matchmaker, Moira. You're not suited for it. Has it ever occurred to you that Russ's bank account won't keep me warm at night?"

Moira jumped to her feet as well and stepped in front of Devon to stop her pacing. "Clay Wyatt and his bank account won't do the job either," she answered bluntly. There was a note of warning in her voice that made Devon freeze and stare at her.

"What's your point?" she asked eventually.

Moira let out her breath on a sigh. "My point is that sooner or later Clay is going to learn the truth about your financial circumstances. And he's not going to overlook them. He's got a problem on that score, Devon—"

"I know."

Moira looked back at her, startled. "Then you're crazier than I thought! If you know about his past, then can't you see that you're in a no-win situation? It's a well-known fact to everyone who knows him that Clay Wyatt has a problem with women and money, though I'd hazard a guess that not many people know why. You're just going to end up getting hurt if you pursue this."

"I'll take my chances."

"Devon, for God's sake!" Moira exploded. "Don't be a romantic little fool! What are you gambling on? That he'll fall in love with you and then it won't matter to him that you're as poor as his ex-wife was when he married her, and a lot poorer than she was when she left him? Forget it!" she warned harshly.

Devon flushed. Give or take a few words, that was exactly what she had decided to gamble on. Why did it sound so stupid when Moira voiced the thought?

Moira noticed her expression and her voice softened, although her words were still blunt. "I've known Clay for five years," she went on. "Believe me when I tell you that he won't fall in love again. He won't allow himself to. He's a loner. It's that simple. What's more, even if you could overcome those staggering odds and he *did* fall in love with you, do you think that's going to make him overlook something that threatens him? Devon, please don't be crazy. Clay Wyatt doesn't overlook things that threaten him. He turns his back and walks away from them. And you'll threaten him. Trust me. You're Gina

69

Wyatt all over again—pretty and poor. That's all he's going to see when he learns the truth."

Devon swallowed painfully against a lump of unshed tears in her throat. The fact of their presence amazed her. She never cried. Was Moira right? Had she fallen head over heels for Clay? Why else would Moira's words have the power to shake her so badly?

Because she knew they were true . . . and she was going to take her chances anyway. She couldn't conceive of doing anything else. It was either that or never see him again.

"Will you lend me the money?" she asked hollowly, not daring to look at her friend.

Moira groaned and dropped down onto the loveseat again. "You're still going to do it, then."

Devon nodded. "I have to."

"You're out of your mind."

"Probably."

Moira sighed and got up to go to the desk in the corner of the room. She wrote a check out quickly and carried it back to her. "You don't have my blessing, you know. I can't stand to see you volunteering your heart up for slaughter like this. But you're my friend, and if you've got your mind made up, I'll help you. Is that all you need?"

Devon looked down at the check, nodded vacantly, then shook her head. "How about a coat and a ride to the airport tomorrow?"

"The ride is easy. Just come over whenever you're ready to leave and I'll drive you to Sky Harbor. But the only coat I've got that's suitable for January in Denver is that chinchilla jacket."

"I'll take it."

Moira laughed suddenly and shrugged. "Well, if you're going to pull this off, I guess chinchilla is the way to go."

Devon bit down on her lip and met her friend's eyes. "It has to be."

5

I cleared up the problem at the hotel. We can go straight to the cabin." Clay paused suddenly as they walked through the terminal and glanced down at her with a contemplative look. "Are you okay?" he asked. "You look a little green around the edges and you haven't said five words since you got off the plane."

Devon forced a weak smile. "I don't like to fly," she answered. "I most especially don't like to fly when it's snowing."

"But you flew up here to see snow."

I flew up here to see you, she thought, but she choked the words back. He seemed so cool and controlled since he'd met her plane, almost as though he were holding himself in check. Which he probably was, she admitted.

"I thought my first and only glimpse of this snow you promised me was going to be at several thousand feet," she responded finally. "For awhile there, I didn't think I'd ever see the ground again. I killed time by writing my obituary."

Clay chuckled softly. For her part, Devon was still

searching for something to smile about. While not exactly caught in the throes of a blizzard, Denver had been bearing up under a sporadic snowfall for hours. At the moment it had stopped again. But her plane had circled the airport for an hour and forty minutes while the runways were cleared and other flights gained clearance to land. The snow had fallen steadily all the while.

"Actually," Clay commented as they left the terminal, "we ought to consider ourselves lucky."

"Lucky? Have you succumbed to cabin fever or something? You don't sound like a sane man."

"Well, we wanted to see snow, and it's snowing, although it hasn't been a very white winter up here so far."

"Until today," she grumbled. "They must have known I was coming. They saved it up for me."

Suddenly he stopped walking. Devon looked up after several steps across the parking lot to find him gone. She turned around with a perplexed frown and walked back to him.

"Is something the matter?"

For a moment, he only stared at her; then his large hand caught her chin and tilted her face gently upward until she found herself caught in those green crystal eyes again. Her heart fluttered. A skittish tremor of awareness passed through her as she waited almost breathlessly for him to say or do something.

"No one knew for sure that you were coming," he answered eventually. His voice was throaty. She shivered slightly at the sound of it; it was so uncharacteristically defenseless. "Least of all myself," he went on. "You really are one of a kind, you know. You keep a man on his toes. The crazy part is, I don't think I mind being on my toes. I don't know how you did it to me, but I'm damned glad you showed up."

Her heart skipped a beat, then started to pound. "I'm glad I did too," she whispered. She stared up into his eyes, unable to break their hold on her. Her awareness of him suddenly became white hot and brought a flush to her cheeks. God, how she wanted this man! Ever since their evening at his hotel, she'd found herself constantly daydreaming of that kiss and yearning for his touch again. And when she was with him or talked to him on the phone, she was obsessed with the quirks of emotion that occasionally shadowed his eyes or his voice. She knew that the odds of becoming a part of his life were one in a million but, staring up into his eyes, she also knew that she had to milk this crazy situation for all it was worth. She had to take the gamble she and Moira had talked about.

She shivered slightly at the magnitude of such an ambition and pulled away from him gently, smiling weakly. "Let's go," she managed. "I think I'd prefer to see this snow from the other side of a car window."

Clay's "cabin" was a three-bedroom house set out in the middle of nowhere. Mountains loomed above it; pines shaded it. It was rustic, she'd allow him that much, but at that point all similarities to a conventional cabin ended. It was a showplace. She'd been bracing herself for an outhouse; she got two and a half baths instead. She'd been prepared to test her culinary skills on a wood stove, but the kitchen was modern enough to put even the one in her old house to shame.

She carried the hot toddy he had made for her over to the picture window in the living room and stared out with a bittersweet smile. She could hear him puttering around in the kitchen, and the sounds left her with an odd sensation in the pit of her stomach. She felt as though they had been holed up in this wilderness hideaway together forever. But by the same token, his chameleonic moods were enough to make him seem like a total stranger. She'd felt as though she'd been walking a tightrope ever since she'd gotten off the plane. He'd been acting like a jungle cat, one who was stalking something that he suspected might do him harm. He inched closer;

he backed away. He watched her carefully and waited. But for what?

She didn't want to think about it. When she finally heard his footsteps on the carpet behind her, she murmured something deliberately innocuous. "It's beautiful, Clay," she said, not bothering to turn around and look at him. "I've always thought that nothing could beat Arizona, but this takes the cake."

"Unfortunately, this weather holds for a good part of the year. It's been known to snow here in May and June. All things considered, I think it's a great place to visit, but I wouldn't want to live here."

He spoke from close behind her. She hadn't realized how close he had gotten. She could feel his warm breath against the back of her neck, and the sensation brought a rosy flush to her cheeks. She caught her breath and nodded out the window, then turned back to him. "You've got horses," she commented, having noticed stables and a pasture off to the left of the house. "Are you as protective of them as Derrick Kendall is?"

At the mention of their first meeting, Clay seemed to relax somewhat. "Not at all," he answered. "You can go climb the fence if you like. Do you ride or do you just like to look at them?"

"Actually, I haven't ridden in years."

"Like skiing?"

"No comparison. I've never fallen down and broken my wrist while I was riding."

"Ah, the truth comes out. You're afraid to ski."

Devon couldn't suppress an ironic smile. "Look who's talking. I prefer to describe my feelings as sensibly cautious. Isn't that the way you put it when we were discussing trust?"

Clay stiffened. The muscles of his shoulders beneath the heavy knit of his sweater seemed to harden before her eyes. Like the jungle cat she had been thinking about all afternoon, he retreated again.

"Well, if we're not going to ski, we ought to do

something typical of a weekend in Colorado," he answered abruptly. "Why don't you go bundle up in something warmer and I'll take you for a ride through the woods. I'll go out and saddle the horses and you can meet me out there."

He was gone almost before he had finished speaking. Devon stared after him as he disappeared into the kitchen. After a moment, she heard the back door open and close. She placed her toddy shakily on a nearby table. Even with him gone and out of sight, a strange tension and anticipation felt tangible in the air. It was as though they both wondered what they were doing there, but neither of them dared to leave before their time together was up. Her whole body seemed filled with a sharp sense of waiting, and she had a hunch she was catching the feeling from him.

Her teeth worked nervously at her lower lip as she went back to the foyer to pick up her overnight bag. She carried it down the hall to the first bedroom and pushed the door open uncertainly. The room was relatively stark, containing only a double bed, nightstand, bureau, and book shelves. It didn't seem likely that it was Clay's room. She dropped the bag on the bed with a sigh and pulled another sweater over the one she already had on. She exchanged her nylon socks for woolen ones, then grabbed Moira's jacket off the coat rack in the hall and headed out to the stables.

One horse was saddled and Clay was working on the other when she joined him. Almost immediately the cold began working on her, and she tugged the collar of Moira's jacket up over her ears as she waited for him to finish.

Clay threw another of his partial smiles in her direction. "You'll warm up after your adrenaline gets going," he promised. "Why don't you wait inside the stables until we're ready? It's warmer in there."

"That," she muttered, "is one of the best suggestions I've heard all day. The other was that hot toddy you offered me. I don't suppose you'd want to skip this whole idea and settle for another?"

"Coward," he teased. He straightened and nodded toward the stables. "Go on, go warm up. You'll change your mind once we get going."

She nodded stoically and moved inside. Hovering near the door, she glanced around. Both Clay's animals and the facilities were excellently maintained. It occurred to her for the first time that he had to have a caretaker or some such thing. But then, why not? Luxuries were only luxuries when you couldn't afford them. It seemed she couldn't get away from reminders that Clay could afford anything he wanted and wasn't about to see it all taken from him again.

Frowning, she started outside again, wanting to stay busy to keep such thoughts out of her mind. Then she caught sight of another horse far back in one of the last stalls and changed direction abruptly. The animal was a sorry-looking gelding who turned his head to inspect her with huge, soft brown eyes. Devon smiled and reached out to stroke his muzzle, but the horse blinked and slowly turned his head away again. The action told her only one thing. He was rarely ridden anymore. He was probably passed by for the sleeker, younger horses. She knew that she was probably being whimsical, but she was convinced that the horse felt too old and too slow to be loved.

Devon turned on her heel abruptly. She found Clay tightening the cinch on the second saddle and hurried over to put a restraining hand on his arm.

"Would you mind saddling a different horse instead?" she asked impulsively.

He glanced down at her, his eyebrows drawing together in a puzzled frown. He looked over his shoulder quickly then turned back to her. "You've invited someone else along?"

"In a manner of speaking. The gelding in the last stall."

Clay's jaw dropped open. "George?"

Devon rolled the name over on her tongue. "George. It fits. Not a very glamorous name, is it? But then, he's not a very glamorous horse. Is he yours?"

"He's mine. But let me get this straight," he answered slowly. "You want to ride George? Of your own free will?"

Devon nodded.

"Instead of Morning Star here?" he went on dubiously. His eyebrows were lifting in that speculative look he had mastered so well.

Devon cast a perfunctory look at the roan mare, then nodded again.

"George won't run, Devon. George won't even trot. You'll be damned lucky if you can get him to walk. You'll be sitting here at the stables when I get back."

Devon shrugged. "I'll take my chances."

Clay ran a hand through his hair in a gesture of total frustration. "I offer you a ten-thousand-dollar piece of horseflesh," he said succinctly, as though he were trying to believe his own words. "And you want to ride a horse that's been standing in line for the bus to the glue factory."

"He's got soulful eyes," she protested. "Sad, lonely eyes, to be more exact. Tell me something. When was the last time anyone rode him?"

Clay pursed his lips together. "My caretaker exercises him once in a while. Sometimes his granddaughter rides him."

"What about you?"

"I haven't ridden him in eight or nine years, I guess." The expression on his face told her that it was something that hadn't occurred to him before.

"I rest my case," Devon responded. "He needs attention. He's probably starving for it. I'm going to give it to him. Do you have any carrots inside?"

"You're going to dangle one in front of his nose? Better bring out the whole bunch."

"I'm going to feed them to him," she answered sourly.

77

"Well, there's probably some in the refrigerator. The caretaker keeps the place pretty well stocked, so—"

"Thanks." Devon nodded eagerly and turned on her heel to go back to the house. She had barely taken a step when he pulled her almost roughly to a stop. Surprised, her eyes flew up to meet his. She saw amazement there, and something else, something tender and warm. It was almost enough to make the snow melt. Her heart stopped and her breath froze in another agonized second of waiting. After a moment's hesitation, he swept her easily into his arms.

"Oh, Devon," he murmured. "You're . . ." He trailed off, looking almost puzzled.

"I'm what?" she asked after a moment.

He shook his head. "Astounding," he finally finished.

His kiss, when it eventually came, was velvety warm, a startling contrast to the frigid air. She had known it was coming, but she hadn't been prepared for the way it was as tender and light as the snow that had begun to fall again. His lips caressed hers in gentle exploration. Devon clung to him, feeling her knees grow weak. She slipped her arms inside his jacket and around his back, but it was over before she knew it. His hands slid down her arms until he held her inches away from him.

She struggled to catch her breath, thinking crazily that he was right. Once her adrenaline got going, the bracing air felt like July in Phoenix—smoldering and moistly hot. She pressed a nervous hand to her lips. They still felt warm with the imprint of his.

"Go get the carrots," he told her huskily, then turned back to unsaddle Morning Star. It was almost as though he regretted acting so impulsively. "I'll take care of things out here," he finished.

Devon nodded and made a blind dash for the house. Now that her heart had finally started beating again, it seemed to thunder. She was shaking and breathless by the time she reached the kitchen. She leaned back against the refrigerator door, her chest heaving.

Finally, she got the carrots and returned slowly, almost hesitantly, to the stables. She wasn't entirely sure what she would find there. She realized for what seemed like the thousandth time that she had no idea what he expected from her that weekend, and doubted if even he knew. She thought again of a jungle cat and shivered.

She didn't look at him as she broke the carrots in half and fed them to the horses. Neither of them spoke until they had mounted and were heading out of the pasture.

"I bought him eleven years ago," Clay said suddenly. His voice seemed unnaturally loud after their long minutes of silence in the snow-muted hills. "He was old then."

"George?" she asked, prompting him more than anything else. She glanced down at the horse. Contrary to Clay's warning, he did walk, albeit slowly.

Clay nodded thoughtfully. His expression was distant. "I still lived in Chicago then. I'd just bought what would ultimately become the Wyatt Penthouse."

"That's the Chicago branch of the chain you've got now?"

He glanced over at her and nodded again. "It was the first of the five. You know, there was something funny about those days. I was comfortable enough financially, more so than I had ever been in my life. I had finally reached the point where I could afford a toy or two. George was a statement, more than anything else. When I was a little kid, I'd read a story about a boy who had a pony. It became something of an obsession with me over the years. I knew I'd know I had made it when I could buy myself a horse." Suddenly his mouth crooked into his partial, cynical smile. "So George was the first toy I bought myself. The ironic part was that I didn't ride, and I didn't dare spend any substantial amount of money on him. Those years in the butcher shop were still too clear in my mind. But the years passed, and I came to realize that riding was something I enjoyed, something that really helped me to unwind, and I was finally able to bring myself to spend the money for younger and finer horses. The thing I wasn't able to bring myself to do was sell George."

"You didn't just not sell him. You must have spent a fortune to have him shipped down here."

Clay slanted a wry smile in her direction. "Sounds crazy, doesn't it?"

Devon shook her head. It took her a minute to find her voice. He might be America's favorite tycoon bachelor, she thought, but he hadn't forgotten the little boy in the tenement. She risked a prayer that when it came time for him to know the truth about her, he would still remember.

But she didn't want to think about their uncertain future at the moment. She didn't dare do anything but take one day, one moment, at a time. And he had asked her a question. "No," she answered softly, "it doesn't."

"Something tells me you've had a George."

She dredged up a smile. "As a matter of fact, now that you mention it . . ." She paused, then explained, "My parents gave me a pony for my tenth birthday. Her name was Ebony. I was something of a loner when I was a kid, and that pony was my best friend through a long stretch of years there. So even when I got too big for her and she started to get old and feeble, I still couldn't bring myself to give her up."

Clay gave one of his soft, warm chuckles. "Sounds familiar. Where is she now?"

Devon's smile, not strong to begin with, faded. "I don't know. I sold her when I moved out here. The vet said that she'd never be able to survive the trip from Boston."

There was a short pause before he changed the subject. "Tell me about your family. Did you have any brothers or sisters to get their noses out of joint when you got a pony for your birthday?"

It was a natural question, but Devon felt a wave of apprehension sweep through her. She didn't trust any conversation that could lead to the topics of her inheritance or Ian.

"I . . . no," she managed in an amazingly calm voice. "I was an only child and spoiled rotten."

"Close to your parents?"

She shot him a wary look that he didn't see. "As close as I could be, considering that I was away at school most of the time."

"Are they still in Boston?"

It was the kind of question she feared. She could feel her pulse beginning to beat erratically in her throat. "They're dead," she answered stiffly. "They were killed in a car accident when I was nineteen."

"I'm sorry. I guess that sounds a little trite, though, coming . . . what? Ten years after the fact?"

Devon swallowed hard and forced a grin. "Watch it, buster. That's eight years. I'm only twenty-seven."

He chuckled again, and amazingly, thankfully, the tension eased out of her. She let out a shaky breath and relaxed a bit in the saddle. It had been another close call, but she'd gotten through it.

Then he spoke again, and she felt another cold knot twist in her stomach. "You said you'd been living in Arizona for eight years. Did you come out after your parents died? And why Phoenix? It's not exactly a stone's throw from Boston."

Her heart sank slowly and nauseatingly into her stomach. It occurred to her suddenly that he might have been fishing when he had asked when her parents had died. Oh, God, she thought wildly, I'm getting paranoid. I'm not cut out for this charade. Her first instinct was to get out of it, to just tell him the truth and get it over with. It would be so simple. She could just tell him that she had married the executor of her father's will and that he had brought her out West. Clay would ask questions, and everything would come out.

But her logic firmly refuted such a possibility. And then what? she asked herself bitterly. Watch him take her back to the house and put her on the next plane? No way. Not yet. She wasn't going to be shoved out of his life without first putting up a fight.

"I got tired of shivering my way through winters," she lied eventually. "I'd heard a lot about southern Arizona's weather and I decided to give it a try. Speaking of which, should we turn around and head back? I never finished my obituary this afternoon. If I'm going to freeze to death, I'd like to do it in style."

"In that jacket, I don't see how you could help it." His voice was easy and smooth again. It had lost its probing edge. Devon uttered another inaudible sigh of relief as he gave Moira's chinchilla a skeptical look. Better to have him questioning that than her past.

"Didn't you bring anything more appropriate for roughing it?" he asked. "That's going to need more than a dry cleaner if you get it dirty."

Don't remind me, Devon thought, cringing inwardly as dollar signs flashed in front of her eyes. Instead she answered, "This is all I have. I rarely venture beyond sunny climates."

He glanced up at the sky, but obligingly turned his horse around. "No sunshine here," he commented eventually.

"I know, but you're worth it." Her response was candid and impulsive. She grinned at him. "Besides, I owe you one. You never turned me over to Derrick that night."

"You've got an amazing memory too." His partial smile flickered for a moment, then faded. In a more serious tone of voice he went on, "I meant what I said back at the stables. You're astounding. You're like a breath of fresh air. I could fall in love with you without even knowing how I did it. Which," he began, then paused to direct another wry smile at her, "is no small feat for someone who doesn't trust women as far as he can throw them."

"By your own admission," Devon murmured. It was all she could do to keep her voice level, but she had to. Her sharp intake of breath had been audible enough. It seemed to echo over the snow-covered land, keeping rhythm with the thundering beat of her heart.

"It doesn't even make sense," he went on. His voice was a murmur, distant and directed inward. Or was it her own ears? She felt as though she were drowning in panic.

"I don't know anything about you," he finished. "I don't know you. All I could tell anyone about you is that you're candid and blunt and you have a penchant for disappearing suddenly." He paused, and his voice came back hushed and intent. "Stop it, Devon. We're beginning to know each other well enough to be able to skip the games. You know about George and Gina and Chicago. Tell me about you and Boston."

Her heart slammed against her chest almost painfully. "Devon," he prodded again, and she jumped at the sound of his voice. Was it time? Did she dare? Their relationship was moving along faster than she had thought it would. When they left the stables, she never dreamed that before they returned he would be talking about love and digging even further into her past. She stared helplessly at George's ears, her expression agonized. Now?

Suddenly she squeezed her eyes shut. No. Not yet. Gambling was only truly dangerous when you were impulsive. She had already come this far. She could wait a little longer until she was sure.

She forced a smile. "You don't want to hear about Boston," she warned him, forcing her voice to be light. "No one really does."

"And why not?" His answering smile was cautious, as though he sensed she was playing with him.

"They regret it and get nervous as soon as they find out I'm a convicted murderess."

It took him a moment, but he finally laughed. "Don't tell me. You're the second coming of Lizzie Borden."

"The Boston Strangler. Please, let's keep our localities straight."

Please, she prayed silently. Let him drop it now.

He didn't.

"There's got to be a real reason you don't talk about yourself. What is it? Bad memories?"

"Some of the worst," she answered honestly enough.

"Your parents?"

"The tip of the iceberg."

"A tragic love affair? Marriage?"

"Stop!" The single word was an anguished command that surprised even herself. Shaking, she reined George to a stop. "Don't, Clay," she went on in a softer voice. "Just don't."

He stopped a few steps in front of her and looked back.

"None of it matters, you know," she went on fervently. "Stop and think about it. What could I possibly tell you that would change what you see right now?"

"That," Clay answered slowly, "is precisely what I'm waiting for you to tell me."

"And I'm asking you how much those kinds of answers can matter. Why can't we just pretend that we were born on the day we met? Why can't we just take it from there?"

Clay looked thoughtful for a moment. "We can . . . if it means that much to you."

Devon took a deep breath that was half relief, half dread. She knew that her very refusal to talk told him that she was hiding something . . . but it was a chance she had to take. It was too early for the alternative. "It does," she answered simply.

Clay shrugged. "In that case, I'll respect your wishes. For now. I can't guarantee that I'll feel that way forever." His eyes burned holes through her. She was beginning to feel sticky and warm beneath Moira's jacket.

"You're so different from anyone I've ever known before," he went on. "You give new meaning to the term woman. I'd like to dig to the bottom of you and find out what makes you tick, and that scares me. I haven't felt that way in a long time. I'm not sure I like the idea of you stopping me."

Suddenly, he turned in his saddle and spurred his horse into a trot that quickly became a gallop. The jungle cat had retreated again. But then, she could hardly blame him. She hadn't given him any reason to venture closer. She took a shaky breath and urged George to follow him.

You give new meaning to the term woman. His words echoed through her brain as she chased after him, and she laughed bitterly, almost hysterically. If he only knew the truth, he would feel so differently.

6

The tension between them was like an invisible unin-
vited guest at a private party. If the air had been alive
with a strange sense of anticipation before they went
riding, now, after dinner, it was virtually singing with
suspense and expectation. Devon stole a look at him
from beneath lowered lashes as she sat on the floor in
front of the fireplace, her back braced against the sofa. At
the moment he was staring into the fire, his face unreada-
ble, although he sat close enough for her to catch every
flicker of emotion in his eyes. But that was just at the
moment. She'd been keenly aware of his scrutiny for
hours.

She moistened her dry lips nervously and cleared her
throat. "You were telling me about Martin Callahan," she
prodded him, trying to pick up the thread of their
conversation again before the silence between them
could grow uncomfortable.

He glanced over at her, his eyes blank for a moment.
She realized that his thoughts had been deep and far
away.

"Right," he answered eventually, his small smile touching his lips again. "Callahan. He used to be an excellent politician, but lately I think he's gotten a little lazy. It's understandable. The family's had vast public support since the days of his father's governorship. He doesn't have to try very hard anymore. But he's still got that Callahan flair and his heart's always been in the right place. He'll keep his seat in the Senate. He's a shoo-in."

"I'm surprised he's running again. I'd heard his health wasn't the best."

Clay nodded absently. It was clear that his thoughts were still elsewhere. "The rumor's cancer. But the last time I saw him, he looked fine. I'm anxious to get a good look at him on the twelfth." Suddenly he fixed her with the intense, scrutinizing look that had been passing in and out of his eyes for hours. "Come with me," he finished abruptly.

Devon frowned at him in confusion. "Where? Did I miss something?"

"No. I guess I didn't make myself very clear. It's something I've been thinking about for hours. I suppose I assumed you were a mind reader in addition to every-thing else." His partial smile was self-effacing now.

Devon offered him a tentative one of her own. "I'm not a mind reader, and I have no idea what you're talking about."

"There's a fund raiser for Callahan on the twelfth. A black-tie affair. It'll probably be boring, but I want you to come with me anyway. I want to see you again."

She laughed nervously. "This weekend's not even over yet. And the twelfth is almost a month away."

He drained his wineglass and sat up to reach for the bottle on the cocktail table, but his eyes never left her. "That's not an answer."

Devon licked her lips nervously and held her glass out to him for a refill. "Do you have to have one from me right now?"

Clay shrugged. "I'd like it."

He'd like it, but she couldn't give it to him. My God,

87

she thought, so much could happen between them in a month. He didn't even know the truth about her yet. She swallowed hard and stalled for time. "Do you always plan dates a month in advance?" she asked, trying to keep her voice light and teasing.

Clay's eyes slid away from her as though he were trying to conceal something. "It's an old habit and hard to break," he answered.

"Could you break it just this once, and just for a few days? I'd like to get back to you on it." She needed time. How could she possibly make a decision now? In the rustic room bathed in the orange glow from the fire, the realities of life seemed so far away. She couldn't make a decision now. She didn't dare.

His eyes came back to her. "I guess I'll have to," he responded. "Even if I don't like it. Now that I've made the decision, I just want you to say yes."

"Seeing me again required a conscious decision?" Again she sought to tease him, and again it was an effort to keep her voice light.

It didn't matter. Clay's probing glance was serious. It lingered on her lips for a moment, then came back to her eyes. "It always does," he murmured at length.

Devon felt her heart skip a beat at his unwavering gaze. "Are we back to caution again?" she asked hoarsely, giving up all pretense of lightness.

"I never left it," he answered honestly enough. "Although you make me think about it." He reached for her hair again, just as he had on the first night she'd met him. His hand brushed against her neck. His touch sent a warm shiver through her.

Yet Devon couldn't help but tense. His words were a warning of things she wanted to forget. She started to straighten up, but his fingers tightened in her hair and he tugged her back again.

"Don't move," he murmured. "Just relax and listen to the wind. Can you hear it howling in the eaves? That's a blizzard you hear out there. It's not worth the effort to move, Devon. You couldn't disappear again if you wanted to, not now."

His thumb began to trace little circles on the smooth skin of her throat. Her flesh tingled. She shuddered slightly. "You're a fine one to talk," she whispered vehemently.

Clay looked surprised, although the stroking movements of his fingers never ceased. "I don't disappear."

"Only mentally," she argued. His hand moved around to the back of her neck. She found it difficult to speak. "You withdraw occasionally."

He was silent for a long minute before he answered. "It's my nature."

"No, I don't think so. Nature is something you're born with. You weren't born with what Gina did to you."

He gazed at her with a look of utter disbelief. "I can't get used to the way you don't mince words."

His eyes were surprised, but they still impaled her. She stared at him as his hand slid away from her neck and down her back. "It's true," she answered shortly. Her words felt dry in her throat.

"I suppose it is," he answered eventually. "I've tried to hold myself away from you. I've tried to convince myself that you're probably just like the others, like Donna and all the other women who are just looking for a free meal ticket. It's difficult."

Her eyes darkened with pain as guilt stabbed at her. She stiffened and looked away. Then his fingers moved further down her spine until they reached the hem of her sweater. Suddenly she felt the warmth of his hand against the small of her back as it slipped beneath the sweater. Warmth flowed through her, melting her tension. It was so easy to forget her lies when he touched her.

"Would you have invited one of the others if I hadn't been able to meet you this weekend?" she asked suddenly, grasping for some semblance of control.

It took him a moment, but Clay finally shook his head. "I've never brought anyone else up here."

"And after I got here, you started wondering if you had done the right thing in asking me."

His smile spread slightly. "You *are* a mind reader."

"Just intuitive and observant. How do you feel now?"

"Does it matter?"

She nodded, trying to do so slowly. She didn't want him to know how very much hinged on it.

"Right now, right this very minute, I feel like making love to you," he answered huskily.

It wasn't the kind of response she had been anticipating. It sent her senses reeling. She almost caught her breath, but the reflex was trapped in a sigh as his persuasive hands slid around to her waist and he pulled her toward him. He lay down on his back, moving her on top of him.

"Clay," she whispered. His name was half moan, half plea.

"Shush," he responded immediately. "We can't go anywhere until the road crews let us out of here tomorrow morning. We're trapped. Let's make the most of it."

"That's not exactly a sterling reason to get ourselves in over our heads."

Again, he contradicted her, stunning her with his perception. "Isn't this what we've been waiting for all afternoon? Wondering if it would happen, if it could or should? It's the next bridge, Devon. Let's cross it and explore what we've got. If it's as good as I think it is, we won't regret it."

His hand moved behind her neck again, guiding her lips down toward his. Their initial contact sent a jolt of longing through her. She moaned low in her throat, and it was a sound of acquiescence. She couldn't have pulled out of his embrace if she had tried. She had been waiting for this moment for what seemed like a lifetime.

His hands slid down her back again and caught her hips. There was a subdued strength in his touch as he held her against him. His mouth was hungry on hers, his kisses almost feverish. Her blood pounded in her brain as she returned the desire that seemed to have exploded in him.

She was losing herself in him. She could feel it happening. Suddenly they were becoming only a man and a woman, without pasts, caught in an elemental, primitive need. That need carried them, obliterating all else. There were no complications, no self-made barriers between them. When he rolled over suddenly, taking her with him and trapping her beneath his hard body, she clung to him. Crushing her beneath him, he took her mouth again with a savage intensity. A strange, delicious heat began simmering within her, and again she moaned his name.

He responded with a quick, urgent movement of his hands. They found the hem of her sweater again and tugged it upward, over her head. They were lying so close to the fire, the orange and crimson light thrown off by the flames danced over her firm, uptilted breasts as he tossed her sweater aside. The warmth of the fire sent currents of heat pulsing over her skin that soon mingled with the fiery friction of his palms sliding over her breasts as he came back to her. Devon gasped over the faint, crackling sound of the fire. She had never known a need so strong as hers was for him at that moment.

He bent his head until his lips touched her nipple with a devastating hesitancy. After the way his mouth had claimed hers, she wasn't prepared for such torturous caution. It was as though a desperate need to take things slowly drove him; he seemed intent upon pausing along the way to make sure that everything felt right and was as it should be. When his tongue finally caressed her sensitive, waiting nipples, she shuddered and buried her hands in his hair, holding him against her. Her greatest fear suddenly had nothing to do with him learning about her lies. She was simply afraid that he would stop.

Wanting to feel his skin against hers, she reached for the hem of his sweater, but her hands shook almost uncontrollably. Her fingers fumbled with the bulky cable knit. Clay kissed the tips of her breasts with almost reverent regret before he straightened away from her and pulled out of his sweater himself.

She wasn't so lost in their shared passion that she didn't have the sense to realize that he might not come back to her, that he might change his mind. She reached out for him and pulled him down to her again, her fingers frenzied as they played across the taut, muscled flesh of his shoulders. She loved the feel of his skin, loved the hard firmness of him. She had dreamed that he would be perfect, and he was.

His hands outlined the circles of her breasts before his tongue finally came back to tantalize their swollen peaks. Then, just as she began to lose herself in the feel of him, he moved away from her again. Devon groaned in protest and reached out to pull him back to her once more. His slight smile pulled at his lips as he shook his head almost infinitesimally and stood up to step out of his jeans, then gently removed hers as well.

She held her breath as she waited for him to come back to her. Then, when he finally did and she felt him flow into her like the heat from the fire, her throat closed in sudden panic. For a brief, agonized moment, her body felt as though it were half ice, half molten warmth. A horrible clarity descended upon her, bitter and cold, as she remembered who she was, who he was, and that the two could never meet easily and peacefully.

Her eyes flew open wide. Now, after this, there could be no turning back. Her lies would be carved in granite; they wouldn't be something to be stumbled over, they would be a brick wall. She opened her mouth in sudden, panicky protest, but Clay silenced her words with another kiss.

"Don't," he cautioned her in a throaty voice. "Don't try to stop now. This is stronger and more important than any doubts. Don't run from me now, Devon. Don't go."

It was only the fact that the encouragement was spoken by him, by a man who was more cautious than she was strong, that enabled her to forget again. She cried out incoherently and melted against him, her tension dissolving. Suddenly their bodies seemed to match in an amazing harmony that defied the differences between them. Reality spun away from her with each of his driving thrusts into her. She felt an almost hysterical need for release climb inside her and fill her. Clinging to him, she cried his name again as a wondrous electricity crackled, then exploded within her.

In the trembling aftermath of their raw need for each other, Clay rolled over onto his side. Devon's eyes flickered open slowly until she found herself caught in the green crystal of his once more. Her hand trembling, she brushed her hair from her eyes, then reached over to gently, tenderly, smooth his as well. She didn't speak. She couldn't. Only one thought whirled through her mind, and it tore at her heart.

Moira *could* be right. And now, more than ever, she couldn't bear to lose him.

7

It was ending. Within the hour, the weekend would be over. And, as though the wrenching disappointment of seeing Clay retreat back to his anonymous house in Tatum Canyon weren't bad enough, Devon had another, more pressing problem to consider. She smoothed the fur of Moira's coat fretfully as their plane touched down on the Sky Harbor runway. Her stomach tightened painfully with apprehension and she grimaced. Clay shot her a curious look, and she gave him a weak smile.

She wasn't cut out for this charade, she thought for the thousandth time. She jumped slightly with nerves as the flight attendant's voice buzzed over the loudspeaker, warning them to stay in their seats until the plane stopped. Before Clay could give her another of his speculative looks, she shrugged quickly and helplessly.

"I told you. I don't like to fly," she explained. It was the first excuse that came to her mind.

Unfortunately, her problem went a lot deeper than that. Any minute now they would be getting off the plane. Clay's Rolls-Royce would be waiting for them.

He'd called his chauffeur that morning and arranged to have it brought to the airport for them.

And now he was expecting to drive her home. But she didn't have the house near Mummy Mountain any longer. She had a tiny apartment in a questionable neighborhood that she didn't dare let him see. Her stomach constricted again until she felt almost ill.

Cunning she wasn't. But how could she have been so outright stupid as to get herself into this predicament? All her planning had gone into getting to Denver and keeping warm while she was there. She had covered her tracks in that area well enough, but now they were back in Phoenix and she hadn't had the foresight to realize that it could turn into a sticky situation. She'd made her return reservation for the four o'clock flight, never stopping to consider that Clay might hold the same reservation. As luck would have it, he had. And he was flying first class. She'd had to dig even further into the money she'd borrowed from Moira to change her seat. She hadn't dared balk at the extra expense of flying first class or allow him to pick up the tab.

Now she didn't have enough money left for a taxi. And even if she had, she knew he wouldn't allow her to take one. She was doomed to go back to her apartment in the Rolls-Royce unless she did some fast thinking. So far, after an hour in the air, she hadn't come up with a single alternative.

Time was running out. They had carried the few pieces of luggage they had in the cabin with them. They didn't have to go to the baggage carousel. They had only to get off the plane, walk through the terminal, and out to the parking lot.

She did some quick calculations. It would take them ten minutes to get to her apartment at the outside. And then her charade would be up. She couldn't bring herself to consider how disastrous the results might be.

"Devon?"

She had been staring out the window, deep in panicky thought. At the sound of Clay's voice, she turned back to him, a startled look in her eyes. As she did, she noticed almost vacantly that the plane had emptied out.

"We can sit here all night and go right back to Denver, but I've got a lot of things to take care of in the morning," he said archly.

She shook her head and forced a smile. "Sorry. I guess I was trying so hard to pretend that we weren't landing that I got caught out in never-never land."

He stood up and began collecting their luggage. Devon squeezed past him, trying not to get lost in the flash of memories that came with brushing up against the hard body that had given her so many glorious moments over the course of the weekend. She had far more important things to consider if she was ever going to touch him again.

And she was. She was more determined about that than ever.

"You don't like to land?" he asked, interrupting her thoughts again as they got off the plane.

She cast him a dark look over her shoulder. "I don't like planes. Period. They're unnatural, you know. If God had wanted us to fly, we'd have been born with wings."

He chuckled. "You surprise me."

"Why?"

"Well, you're obviously a lady of some leisure. And I assumed that you still have some family in Massachusettes. I guess I figured that you fly a lot, and that doing it a lot, you'd have gotten used to it—even if it's not your favorite pastime."

Devon nearly stumbled as they crossed the terminal. Her heart leaped into her throat and she had to talk around it as she gave great attention to her toes. "No, I . . . I don't fly much," she mumbled in response, biting her lips to avoid adding, "Not anymore."

"That's obvious," he responded dryly. They pushed through the doors and stepped outside. Devon realized suddenly and with a sick feeling that her time was running out faster than she'd thought. The Rolls-Royce was at the curb waiting for them. Clay greeted his chauffeur and reached for the overnight bag that she held clenched in her hand. She gave it up regretfully.

Within minutes, their luggage was stashed in the trunk and he was holding the door open for her. Devon worked hard to conceal a despairing look and slid into the back seat.

Everything seemed to be going in slow motion. Every action seemed to be drawn out and threatening. She watched the chauffeur get into the front seat and start the engine. Her eyes flew back to Clay as he got into the car beside her. And then, inevitably, the question came.

"Where to?"

Her breath caught in her lungs. Her mind worked frantically. The world went still. After one precious weekend, she was going to lose him. Telling him the truth would be bad enough. Springing it on him like this would be disastrous.

"Devon? We're not in a plane, and we're not landing. What's wrong with you?"

She struggled to take a deep breath. She felt as though she were gasping, but no sound came. Then, amazingly, a solution sprang into her mind. It wasn't a good one. It wasn't believable. It was risky. But it was a solution, and anything was better than going back to her apartment.

She whirled on him, praying that her eyes looked startled. "Oh, damn!" she exclaimed.

If anyone looked startled, it was Clay. "What's the matter?"

"Nothing. Everything. I just remembered something."

"Something that's going to bring the world to an end?"

"Something that's liable to bring my friendship with Moira to an end," she lied, trying to sound convincing. "I promised her that I'd have dinner with her and Derrick tonight. I completely forgot about it."

Clay frowned at her briefly. She held her breath until his slight smile touched his lips again. "That's understandable, I guess," he answered. "You've had your mind on other things this weekend."

She smiled at him softly before her thoughts turned back to the dilemma she was in. She glanced down at her watch. "It's only six-thirty," she murmured doubtfully. "Maybe I could still make it if you dropped me off there."

Clay's eyebrows rose. "Is it worth it? Why don't you just call her when you get home and explain?"

Why, indeed? she asked herself frantically. "I, uh . . . oh, we've been planning this thing for weeks. It would be rude to cancel out on her now."

Clay shrugged, but his expression was beginning to turn dark with doubt. "Okay," he answered eventually. "I'm not sure I understand, but we'll do this your way. Miguel?" The chauffeur glanced over his shoulder at him. "We're going to Scottsdale. The Kendalls' place. You remember where that is?"

Miguel nodded silently and Clay turned back to Devon. "Sooner or later I'm going to get to see your new house. Do you realize I haven't been there yet? It seems preposterous when you think about it."

Devon's heart stopped beating. The smile she turned on him felt brittle. *Her new house.* That was a joke. "No more preposterous than the fact that I haven't been to your house yet," she managed to answer.

Clay's expression became guarded. She sensed that she had touched a nerve again somehow, but she couldn't help but feel relieved. At least it would get his mind off the topic of where she lived.

"Well, as I said, I don't socialize much," he responded at length. "Not many people *have* been to my house. It's more or less my private domain."

"Is that a polite way of telling me I'm not invited?" she prodded him deliberately, trying to keep his thoughts occupied.

The look he gave her was tender enough to make her guilt churn inside her again. Oh, God, what was she doing to this man?

"No, it doesn't mean that at all," he answered slowly. "We'll have dinner there some night this week."

Devon took a deep breath and prodded him again. "This week? Not next month?"

His expression was both pained and exasperated. "Need I remind you that Rome wasn't built in a day?" he asked. Then he became serious, his voice soft. "Don't push me, Devon. This is all new enough to me as it is."

She nodded miserably. Fresh guilt mushroomed within her at the way she had deliberately poked at his sore spots to keep his mind off the subject of where she lived. "New," she whispered in response, "and somewhat frightening too, I suppose, considering your experiences at the hands of women."

He cast her a perfunctory, guarded glance, then looked out at the street. "Not frightening," he answered shortly. "Just worrisome and thought-provoking. Here we are."

She grimaced at the tightness in his voice and looked up to find that they had stopped in front of Moira's house. It was time to say good-bye. Her frown deepened. Well, she consoled herself, at the very least, she had no reason to believe that good-bye would be forever. An odd mixture of relief and disappointment washed over her. She sighed and turned to him, but he was already getting out of the car.

"I'll walk in with you," he said. "I haven't seen Derrick and Moira in a few weeks. I'd like to say hello."

Sudden, surging panic filled her throat again. There was no way to argue that one, not without making an incomprehensible scene. But Derrick and Moira had no idea that she was coming.

She got out of the car and slowly followed him up the walkway, her thoughts whirling. With any luck, Moira would answer the door and catch on quickly. The odds were against their maid doing it; she lived in, but it was Sunday, and even live-ins had days off. But what if Derrick came to the door? She'd ask for Moira. Derrick would think she was out of her mind, but there was nothing else she could do. She closed her eyes briefly and prayed as Clay reached for the brass knocker on the door.

Moira answered. The relief that flooded her was so strong that she thought her knees would buckle beneath her.

She stepped forward quickly until she stood in front of Clay and gave Moira a desperate look. "Am I late? Are we going to have my head on a silver platter for dinner? I'm sorry—we were in Denver, just got back, and I forgot all about our plans. I got here as early as I could."

A brief flash of surprise, almost infinitesimal, showed in Moira's eyes. Devon could only hope that Clay hadn't seen it. "Uh, no," Moira answered, too awkwardly for Devon's peace of mind. "We weren't planning to eat until later. It's okay."

"Oh, good. I couldn't remember what time you'd told me to be here."

Moira recovered quickly. Her ensuing smile was smooth and bright. "I don't think we set a time, did we? Come on in." She turned her smile on Clay, and Devon could have kissed her. "How have you been, stranger? It's got to be weeks since we've seen you."

They moved into the foyer. Clay shrugged and looked down at Devon. Nothing in his eyes betrayed that he might be suspicious. "Moira doesn't know the meaning of forgiveness. If I commit one social gaffe, I hear about it for years." He turned back to Moira. "I haven't called because I've been busy. Is that a satisfactory excuse?"

Moira grinned. "It'll have to do. Of course, you can always make up for it by staying to have dinner with us."

Clay feigned a look of fear. "I can't. I suppose this means I'm going to be in the dog house for another year?"

"It depends on your excuse."

"I've got a call coming in at seven o'clock from my comptroller for the San Francisco hotel."

"On a Sunday night?" Moira gave him a disbelieving look.

"Hotels know no holidays. Sorry, but thanks anyway." He turned back to Devon and touched her arm softly. Even with the suspense that coiled in her stomach as she listened to their exchange and prayed that Moira wouldn't slip up, his touch moved her. Warmth flooded her as he trailed his fingers up her arm and touched her cheek. "I'll call you," he said simply; then, after a rush of good-byes from Moira, he slipped out the door.

Devon had no time to ponder about the way the foyer suddenly felt empty without his presence. As soon as the door shut behind him, Derrick emerged from the study.

"Did I hear Clay's voice?" he asked.

Moira shot him a withering look. "If you had removed your nose from those blueprints five minutes sooner, you might have had a chance to say hello to him."

Devon interrupted them quickly. "It doesn't matter. I think he was in a hurry. That phone call . . ." She trailed off and reached out to squeeze Moira's hand. "Thanks for getting me out of that."

Moira's frown and subsequent shake of her head were both resigned. "The least you could have done was warn me."

"There wasn't time. He was going to take me home. I couldn't think of a way out of it until we got into the car, and then I thought of you."

Neither of them noticed Derrick's confused look. Moira shook her head again. "Well, it was a close call. I know I said I'd help you, but this is getting ridiculous. Do you realize that if he *had* stayed for dinner, we would have ended up with pastrami sandwiches? Derrick and I have to deliver blueprints to a new client first thing in the morning, and there have been problems all the way through the whole project. We were going to work right through dinner and grab sandwiches along the way. I'd like to have seen us explain *that*."

Devon smiled weakly. "We would have thought of something, I'm sure. You were marvelous."

Moira finally grinned. "What can I tell you? I'm brilliant. Anyway, as long as you're here, how about a pastrami sandwich and a cold bottle of beer? It'll give me one more chance to try to talk some sense into you. Brilliant or not, I'm not sure I can go through this again."

Derrick broke into their conversation suddenly. "Do I want to know what's going on here?" he asked doubtfully.

Neither Devon nor Moira looked at him. "No," they said flatly in unison.

"Something tells me that's the best news I've heard all day." He shrugged and turned back into the study again.

Devon started backing toward the door. "Listen, thanks for the offer of a bite to eat, but I think I'd rather go home. I can't thank you enough for that rescue mission."

Moira nodded. "I know. Okay, have it your way. You always do anyway." She followed her to the door. "Your car's out in the garage, and the keys are in it. Derrick moved it in there for you. There was extra space because the Jaguar's in the shop. Body work. Someone backed into it and took a headlight out. I should tell you that I've been running around in your Rabbit all weekend, so don't worry about the money you owe me. I took it out in mileage and gas."

"Moira, don't—"

"Oh, can it. You need help in more areas than just Clay Wyatt. Let me do what I can. Just give me my coat back and get out of here."

Devon squeezed her eyes shut briefly as she shrugged out of the chinchilla. A hard lump of exhausted tears seemed to be clogging her throat. "Moira," she tried again, "I don't—"

"Know what to say?" Moira finished for her. "Just forget about it, will you? I've got the money and you don't. Besides, you ought to save your talking for Clay Wyatt." Her voice was suddenly serious. "I mean it, Devon. I saw the way he looked at you tonight. Your time's running out. You've got to tell him, and you've got to do it soon. I can't keep coming to your rescue forever. Clay's my friend too. After a certain point, I'm going to have to back out of this game."

Devon gave her a stricken look. "I know. I'll think about it."

Think about it? She hadn't done anything else for weeks, she thought as she walked through the cool twilight toward the garage. And it wasn't getting any easier to come to a decision. If anything, she dreaded it more.

By the time she let herself into her apartment, the hard lump of tears in her throat had faded away, but it left her with an empty feeling. Exhaustion, both physical and mental, overwhelmed her. She was so tired her bones seemed to throb. Moira was right; she couldn't keep this up much longer, but whether for Clay's sake or her own was a distinction she couldn't make. She knew only that her fatigue went deeper than just the tiring chore of keeping Clay from learning the truth all weekend. It had been growing for a year, a year spent paying for one single mistake. She was tired of scrambling to pay bills, she was tired of having to accept Moira's charity, but most of all, she was tired of all the stress and unhappiness. Sudden fury erupted in her as she thought of all that Ian had robbed her of, and she started to shake. For the first time in a year, she truly despised him. She had always forbidden herself to feel anything regarding him whatsoever—after all, there was nothing to be gained from bemoaning the past—but now she allowed herself the luxury of hating him. She'd given up the furs and the furniture, the house and the cars. She'd given him a good chunk of her self-respect, her naiveté, and all the financial security she'd ever had. She was *not* about to let him take Clay Wyatt away from her, too.

She went to the kitchen and rummaged through the cabinet over the sink for the precious bottle of bourbon she kept there. She rarely touched it, but tonight she figured she deserved it. She fixed herself a drink with hands that still trembled slightly and went back to the living room, tucking the bottle under her arm.

There was a way out of this, a way to salvage Clay's emotions, her pride, *and* their relationship. There had to be. It was just a matter of brainstorming the situation long and hard until she came up with a solution. But how did you tell a man with whom you were on the verge of falling in love that you were all the things he feared most?

She woke up ten hours later, still without a solution. The bottle of bourbon sat untouched on the coffee table. Her drink sat beside it, half full. Her neck was stiff from sleeping in such an awkward position on the sofa, and as she sat up, she shrugged her shoulders slowly and painfully. She hadn't brainstormed anything the night before. As soon as her head had touched the cushions of the sofa, she'd fallen asleep. All her problems still remained.

But the light of day had a way of making things seem easier. She stood up and stretched, then started to clean up the remnants of her abortive thinking session. She might not have all the time in the world, but she did have a little time yet. She'd think of a way to tell Clay the truth—*after* she thought of a way to pay for the supplies she would need to cater the party she had scheduled for the following night. She took it for granted that her supplier would refuse to extend her credit for another week.

She passed by the telephone answering machine on her way to the kitchen and frowned down at it. The little signal light told her it had been taking calls. She hadn't remembered to play it back the night before. Some splurge this gadget had turned out to be, she thought, flipping the switch to let it play back the messages. She'd bought it second-hand after the day she had sneezed in Clay's ear during her mimicked recording, but it was a luxury so new to her that she continually forgot to check it.

As she washed out her glass from the night before and stored the bourbon away again, various creditors complained about the fact that they hadn't received checks from her. She didn't bother to write the numbers down. She knew them all by heart. Then a new voice filled the room and she paused, drying her hands slowly and thoughtfully as she stared at the machine and listened.

"My name is Bill Murdock, Ms. Jordan. I'm with Senator Callahan's election committee. Your name was given to me by Luke Myers in regard to catering an affair we're having next month. If you could give me a call first thing Monday morning at 555-1660, I'd much appreciate it."

Devon sat down slowly on one of the kitchen chairs and closed her eyes. A vision of an hourglass running out of sand was all she could see.

8

~~~~~~~~~~~~

She had known, of course. She had known that the
"affair" Bill Murdock had spoken of could be none other
than the Callahan fundraiser Clay had invited her to. Fate
would have it no other way.

Devon hung up the telephone slowly after placing her
return call to Murdock. She collapsed against the back of
her chair, feeling the fight drain out of her. It was over.
Talk about mixed blessings, she thought bitterly. Her
heart squeezed painfully in despair. The Myers' party at
the beginning of the month had done exactly what she
had prayed it would do. It had gotten her referred to the
right people. The Callahan fundraiser was precisely the
big job she needed so desperately. Murdock had talked
of hosting five hundred people. The chance to cater it
was everything she had dreamed of and worked for . . .
and now she dreaded it.

Hot tears—undoubtedly the same ones she had
choked back the night before—finally glistened on her
eyelashes. She wiped them away irritably but couldn't

stem their flow. Finally, she crossed her arms on the table and rested her head against them as the tears slowly found their way down her cheeks and splattered the pile of bills in front of her.

She was trapped.

She couldn't turn the job down. She needed the money, the chance, too desperately. But taking it would mean telling Clay the truth. Not later, but now. He'd be there. With or without her by his side, he'd be there. If she didn't tell him, he'd find out anyway. It was best coming from her, right from the horse's mouth.

She shuddered at the thought and straightened up, her mind going automatically to a frenzied search for alternatives. But she knew there weren't any. Not this time. If she hadn't learned anything else from her childish naïveté concerning Ian, she had learned that before she could worry about romance, she had to worry about taking care of herself. It had been a long, horrible year. Her affair with Clay was so tentative, so iffy, she couldn't risk her very existence on it. And the fact remained that whether he turned his back on her or forgave her, she still had to pay her rent and eat.

She had to take the job.

Her throat ached with defeat as she stood up and reached for the telephone again. There wasn't going to be any easy way to tell him. If she put it off and tried to plan it, she'd never be able to bring herself to do it. Holding her breath, she dialed the number of Clay's office.

His secretary's voice left no doubt to the fact that Devon was hardly the first woman who had called and asked for her employer.

"Your name please?" she asked abruptly.

"Devon Jordan. Is he—"

"He's unable to come to the telephone right now."

"I was just going to ask you how long you think he's going to be tied up."

The secretary sighed dramatically. "I'm afraid I really

can't tell you that. I'll give him your message and we can both hope for the best." She didn't have to tell Devon that she had been through this before and knew that if Clay didn't call Devon back, she would keep calling him.

"Thank you." Devon replaced the telephone again and ran her fingers through her hair fretfully. She had to keep busy while she waited for him to return her call. If she had time to think, she would go mad. Worse, she would chicken out. She grabbed a cookbook from the kitchen counter and dropped it onto the table with a thud. She had the finishing touches to put on the menu for the party the next night. That should keep her occupied enough. Maybe.

But no sooner had she sat down again and flipped the book open than the telephone rang. The color drained from her face as she jumped up and glanced over at it. Three rings. Four. *Answer it,* she commanded herself. *Pick up the damned phone and get it over with.*

She reached for the telephone, feeling as though she were reaching for a noose to hang herself with.

"Devon?" Clay's voice was warm, if a bit hurried. "What's up?"

She felt a brief flash of elation at his attentiveness in calling her back so quickly. Then it crumbled, disintegrating and scattering like ashes caught in the wind. He'd probably never call her again.

She searched for her voice. A suffocating despair seemed to have closed off her vocal chords. "I, uh . . ." She paused, then tried again. "You ran out of Moira's so fast last night that I didn't have the chance to thank you."

"Thank me?"

For one of the best weekends of my life. She forced herself to rephrase the thought. "For a great weekend," she answered.

She could hear him giving her that partial smile in the ensuing silence. "No thanks are necessary," he answered eventually. "Didn't you notice that I enjoyed myself as much as you did?"

"The possibility did occur to me." Her voice sounded hoarse, not at all normal, even to her own ears.

"Well, I appreciate the call anyway. It's a nice touch, but then, you're full of them."

"Nice touches?"

"The nicest."

Desolation swept over her. He wouldn't feel that way for long. She cleared her throat again and answered, "How do you feel about another one?"

"Another weekend or another nice touch?"

"The latter. I'd like to take you out to lunch." She knew suddenly that she couldn't do this over the telephone. If she were going to tell him the truth, she had to do it in person. If she stood any chance at all of having him forgive her, it lay in being close to him and appealing to whatever feelings he had for her.

Clay's voice was amused when he answered. "What for?" he asked.

"To thank you for a great weekend, of course."

"You don't have to do that. I told you, no thanks are necessary."

Devon took a deep breath and struggled to sound nonchalant. "Have you won the Chauvinist of the Year award yet?"

This time he laughed outright. "No, but I suppose you're going to tell me that I'm in the running for it."

"Bingo. If I did something nice for you, wouldn't you want to reciprocate?"

"Sure. What's your point?"

"I want to reciprocate. I shouldn't lose the chance simply by virtue of my gender."

There was another short silence. "I guess I never considered that the equality of the sexes might extend to who picks up the tab for meals," he answered finally.

"I think there are a lot of things you haven't considered before, at least where women are concerned," she muttered.

"But you're going to tell me about them, I'm sure."

"Not right now. I think we should take them one at a time, beginning with lunch."

Clay sighed resignedly, but she sensed that he was smiling. "Okay. Where and when?"

"How about noon at the zoo?"

She had expected him to balk at the place, but it was the time that seemed to trip him up. "Today?" he asked.

"Can you do it?"

"Just a second." She could hear him flipping through his calendar. Fresh despair turned the pain in her stomach into gnawing agony. If he couldn't see her today, if she couldn't tell him the truth today, she'd never be able to bear the waiting.

"Sure," his voice came back. She couldn't decide whether she was destroyed or relieved. "I can make it today as long as we do it early. You said noon?"

"Is that early enough?"

"It's fine." He paused, then came back with the response she'd been expecting. "You want me to meet you at the zoo?"

Devon took a deep breath. "That's right. There's a snack bar and some picnic tables right inside the main gate. You can't miss them. They've got the best hot dogs in Phoenix."

"Hot dogs," he repeated.

"Hot dogs. I'll see you at noon."

She hung up quickly before he had the chance to try to talk her out of it. With any luck, she thought, he'd see that they could enjoy themselves as much with hot dogs at the zoo as they could if they dined in the finest restaurant in Phoenix.

Besides, it was all she could afford.

The bench of the picnic table was hard and uncomfortable, and Devon shifted on it restlessly. She glanced down at her watch. Five of twelve. It had been five of twelve ten minutes ago too. She was sure of it. Time was crawling. Her pulse pounded and she felt weak from nerves. She held her wrist to her ear and listened to hear if her watch was still ticking. Had it broken? Was it really twelve-thirty? Had he stood her up?

She glanced up at the main gate again, and this time she spotted him. Panic began rioting within her as though someone had flipped a switch. She clenched her fists in her lap until she felt her nails bite into her palms, then realized what she was doing and forced herself to relax. So much hinged on how she handled this.

Some small part of her had suspected that he would look out of place and incongruous at the zoo. He didn't, not really. He certainly didn't look like a tourist, not in his three-piece suit, but neither did he look out of place. It was that air he carried himself with, she decided. It was the way he walked, with authority and indifference that said clearly that he didn't give a damn if anyone wondered why he was at the zoo when he clearly looked as though he should have been at a board meeting. He was so fascinating, so perfect.

Don't think about it.

She worked deliberately to clear her mind of its panicky hodgepodge of thoughts as she stood up to meet him. He was wearing his peculiar partial smile, and amusement glittered in his eyes.

He bent to kiss her. Devon closed her eyes and tried to steady herself against the impact the simple gesture had on her. Would it be the last time?

He straightened and glanced around. "You know, I'm beginning to think this was a great idea. Leave it to you. I don't think I've been to a zoo since I was a teenager. My parents had signed me up for some project for impoverished kids. They used to try to get us out of the city in the summer so we wouldn't make trouble. I think the only trip I remember is the zoo. I was thinking about that after you called." He broke off and looked down at her. His expression was somewhat troubled. "There I go again. I constantly seem to find myself telling you the story of my life." Abruptly he changed the subject. "So where are these fantastic hot dogs you promised me?"

Devon swallowed hard. Maybe doing this in person

hadn't been the best idea after all. His proximity, coupled with the knowledge of what she had to tell him, seemed to be paralyzing her. She shook her head as though to bring herself back to her senses and struggled to find her voice. "I, uh . . . over there." She pointed toward the snack stand, but when Clay made a move toward it, reality seemed to flood back in on her. Immediately she was alert, moving, functional again.

She put a restraining hand on his arm. "Oh, no, you don't. Just sit down. This is my treat. I'll go get them. What do you want on yours?"

He sat down on the bench slowly and gave her a baffled look. "You're really going to buy?"

"You expected me to invite you out here and then play docile little games while you get all gallant and pick up the tab?"

He stared at her hard for a moment. "Yes," he answered eventually.

"Well, as I mentioned earlier, you've got a lot to learn." *That* was the understatement of the year. She shook her head again, refusing to think about it. "What do you want on yours?" she asked again.

"Well, as long as I'm tripping down Memory Lane, I might as well do this right. Everything. If you see it on the counter, pour it on there."

She forced a smile and went to get the hot dogs. Following his instructions, she loaded his with everything from catsup to onions. She settled for mustard on hers. She doubted she'd be able to eat it anyway.

She watched carefully as he took his first bite. "Well? What do you think?"

Clay chewed thoughtfully. "You're right. It's a great hot dog." Then suddenly his expression became speculative. "But it's still a hot dog. Are you trying to make a point with all this?"

Devon felt the world beginning to fade away. The sounds of the children around them died. The tempting aroma from the snack stand behind them dissipated. She shifted on the bench again, feeling light-headed and weak.

It was the perfect opening. And she had to take it.

She forced herself to nod. "I . . . actually, yes."

He looked surprised. "You *are* trying to make a point? I thought maybe this was just another case like the day you wanted to ride George. I'm never sure with you."

"Well, it is, sort of . . . like George. Actually, I have to talk to you, and I thought this would be a good way to . . ." She trailed off. To what? Prove to him that money wasn't everything? Not an auspicious way to begin her confession, she decided.

She tried again. "There's something I've got to tell you," she began, coming to the conclusion that the beginning, as always, was the best place to start.

He wasn't making things any easier. He stared at her silently, his jaw working as he chewed his hot dog.

"Do you remember when you asked me how it was that I came to Phoenix all the way from Boston?" she blurted.

"You came out here with the zoo?"

It seemed to her that he was deliberately trying to make light of the situation, as though he sensed what was coming and didn't want to hear it. Devon shook her head vehemently. Her adrenaline pumped through her violently. Now that she had started, she was going to finish.

"I came out here with my husband," she answered bluntly. "I was married when I first moved to Phoenix. And I was married when—"

"What does this have to do with the fact that we're eating at the zoo?" His question was terse, his eyes guarded and angry. Devon felt sick.

"It doesn't, but—"

"Then let's talk about the zoo, shall we?" His voice was growing colder.

"What's the matter with you?" she demanded. So far, she had said nothing that would threaten him. Or had she? She didn't know. All she could be sure of was that

113

this wasn't starting out well. A dull ache of foreboding clutched her heart.

Suddenly the anger went out of Clay like air from a balloon. He pushed his paper plate away and massaged his temples, looking confused. "I'm sorry," he muttered. "I don't know what's the matter with me." He glanced up to meet her searching eyes. "But I guess we're going to sit here all day until I figure it out and tell you, right?"

She frowned at him in silence, not knowing what to say.

"Well," he went on abruptly, "I haven't got all day, so I guess we ought to get to the bottom of this now. I guess I just don't like thinking about you belonging to someone else. I've never thought of you in those terms. God, I know you're twenty-seven years old, I know you've had lovers, maybe even a husband . . . but that doesn't mean I have to deal with the fact. I never thought about it before, but I guess the fact is that I've been turning my head the other way, playing ostrich, whatever. And I want to keep it that way." He offered her a small smile. "So if this ex-husband of yours is what—" He broke off suddenly, looking appalled. "He *is* an ex?"

Devon nodded dully. She couldn't give him much, but she could give him that.

Clay relaxed. "Thank God. Well, then, if he's what you wanted to talk to me about, I'd just as soon drop the subject," he went on. "Weren't you the one who suggested that we pretend we were born on the day we met? I'm beginning to think that's an excellent idea."

She stared down at her untouched hot dog. Misery felt like a steel weight pressing against her chest. She could scarcely breathe. He wanted to change the subject . . . but she couldn't do that. She had to get this out. It was time.

And he was already reacting badly. Hope drained out of her. She felt hollow.

"There's more," she answered in a strangled voice. "If you want to be precise about it, I was really born roughly three days after the first time we met."

"Close enough," he responded. His voice was a growl that was growing threatening again.

"No, it's not. Precision is important here. It means that—"

"Damn it, Devon!" he exploded. Heads turned to stare at them but, as usual, he neither noticed nor cared. "I don't want to hear about it. Didn't you listen?"

"Yes, but—"

"But nothing! I don't want to hear about the man you were married to. I can't make it any plainer than that. How would you like to sit here and listen to me eulogize my ex-wife?"

"I was hardly eulogizing Ian!" she snapped heatedly, but the anger drained out of her as fast as her hope had. She slumped against the picnic table, covering her face with her hands. A choked, almost hysterical laugh escaped her. He was right. She didn't want to hear any more about Gina, didn't want to think of him belonging to anyone else. Something subtly possessive had crept into her feelings for him. She wasn't sure when it had happened, but it had. Oh, God, she thought desperately, what a double-edged sword this had turned out to be! She had waited until he felt something for her before telling him the truth, and now it seemed that they both felt too much.

It was both reason to shut up and reason to keep talking. What she had been hiding from him could alter their entire relationship. And if he didn't want to listen now, how would he feel in another month?

She looked up at him again with pleading eyes. "Please, Clay," she whispered. "Please just listen to me." When he didn't protest immediately, she rushed on. "When I said I thought we ought to pretend we were born on the day we met, I meant it. It seemed like a good idea then. But several years ago believing in Santa Claus was a good idea too, and that changed. I grew up and understood that I had to put my belief in more concrete things, not fantasies. Our relationship has grown too. Just as you reach a point where you've got to stop trusting in make-believe, we've reached a point where we've got to start being realistic. I've changed my mind about talking about our pasts. I think they're important now. They reflect the people we've become, what we are to each other."

Clay stared at her enigmatically for a moment, then scowled. "Whoever said women were unpredictable certainly hit the nail right on the head. Do you realize that you came up with this day-we-were-born philosophy less than seventy-two hours ago?" He looked up at the sky in exasperation for a moment, then turned back to her. His expression made the last of her hope shrivel and die.

"And now you've changed your mind," he went on. "I liked your first philosophy better, Devon. The hell with being realistic." His tone was final. As he finished speaking, he got to his feet. "Let's just forget we had this conversation, shall we? Just pretend it didn't happen? It's getting late and I have to run."

She wasn't going to be able to tell him. He wouldn't listen. She glanced up at him with a stricken expression that had nothing to do with his leaving.

He misread her look. "Devon, I'm sorry," he murmured, pulling her to her feet and into his arms. His kiss was brief but warm. Still, it couldn't thaw the icy spot in her heart.

"I agreed to go to a party this afternoon before you called me to meet you for lunch," he explained. "It's the Carlsons' fiftieth anniversary bash. They're renewing their vows, or some such thing, and it's scheduled to start at two o'clock. I've got to go. I had my secretary run out and buy a gift, and I've got to stop by the office and pick it up."

"It's okay," she answered hollowly.

His eyes searched hers. It was obvious that he didn't believe her, but brightness was something she simply couldn't achieve at the moment.

"Look, I'll call you about getting together for dinner this week," he tried again.

"Fine."

"Devon, damn it—"

"Go to your party," she interrupted him softly, struggling to smile. "I'll talk to you later." She dropped down onto the bench again and reached for her purse.

Clay nodded hesitantly, then turned on his heel and started for the gate. After a few steps, he stopped and turned back to her. "By the way," he called out. "Have you had a chance to come up with an answer for me about that fundraiser for Callahan?"

Her breath froze. Her lungs felt as though they would burst. She scarcely managed to shake her head. "For God's sake, Clay! It's a month away!" she finally exploded. Then remorse flooded her. He couldn't possibly understand why the last thing she wanted to think about was that fundraiser.

She shook her head. "Sorry. I, uh . . . I'll check my calendar when I get home. I'll let you know as soon as I can."

As soon as you'll let me, she thought bitterly, but there was no chance that she could say the words aloud. Clay gave her another brief smile and headed toward the gate again.

She watched helplessly as he disappeared. He had been gone a long time before a new thought managed to penetrate the sick feeling of failure that filled her.

He wasn't going to the Carlsons' anniversary party alone.

She didn't know how she knew, but she knew. Jealousy, possessive and strong, pulled at her heart. She drew her breath in sharply, briefly. She was sure that he would have invited her rather than go alone. But he hadn't invited her. He had invited someone else.

She was suddenly, vehemently glad that she hadn't been able to tell him the truth. Contrary to all his talk about not wanting to think of her belonging to anyone else, their relationship wasn't half as close as she had thought it was. Not yet. If he was still seeing other

women, then he couldn't care enough for her to forgive
her.

It *was* too soon, after all. She still had time. The
fundraiser was, as she had told him, still a month away.
She got up from the bench, feeling an odd mixture of
relief and pain. She'd been given a reprieve.

Or had she been given a sentence?

9

It was amazing how things that could tear your heart out one day became almost insignificant in the face of new problems the next. Maybe, she thought, she was just having a nervous breakdown. Maybe her brain was on overload. Quite possibly it had too much to think about, so it had simply shut down.

Any way she looked at it, Clay became a distant, dark ghost on the fringes of her mind as Devon leaned over the cash register. She gave the short, balding man behind the counter a pleading look. "Joe, please. If you'll just let me take this stuff now, I swear on my life that I'll bring you a check first thing in the morning. It's all for a party I'm doing tonight."

The man frowned at her and shook his head doubtfully. "I seem to remember that you said that same thing the last time. I didn't see any money for a week."

"But you got it, didn't you? And I *did* come back the next day to explain what had happened. Those people were from out of town. They gave me an out-of-town

check. I had to wait for it to clear before I could pay you."
When his expression didn't waver, she was forced to throw her pride out the window. "Please, Joe. I need your help. If I don't do this party tonight, I don't pay the rent."

"Can't you do the party without booze?"

She scowled at him. "Please. I didn't know I'd have to plead with you to be realistic too."

Joe shook his head wearily. "Okay, okay. Take it. But I mean it, Devon. One week, that's all I'm giving you. I don't see any money by next Tuesday, you don't ever take anything on credit again. You got it?"

Devon let out a sigh of relief and started putting the bottles into bags. "I got it," she said. She hefted a bag on each hip. "And Joe, thanks. Again."

"The missus thinks I'm having some kind of fling with you or something," he grumbled. "I don't do this for nobody else. In this day and age, a fellow—"

"I've been living next door to you for a year, Joe," she cut him off. "You know I'm not going anywhere. And you know you'll get your money." She gave him an encouraging smile and turned toward the door. "See you in the morning."

By the time she reached the door, her thoughts had already left Joe and his liquor. They swerved back to Clay, plucking him from the fringes of her mind again and plunking him down dead center. She was remembering the look on his face when he told her not to talk about Ian and thinking that it was the first time she'd ever seen him lose his cool when she heard someone call her name.

She paused, looking around the liquor store with a blank expression. It took her several seconds to put Clay away in the back of her brain again and focus on the tall, lanky man walking around one of the displays and heading toward her.

Russ Sumner. Wouldn't Moira love this, she thought dismally. Their conversation the day before she had gone to Denver hadn't been the last time Moira had tried to push him on her. Devon wondered briefly where his mother was as he walked toward her. The standing joke was that the man never went far without her.

She dredged up a polite smile. "Hi, Russ. What are you doing in this neck of the woods?" He lived in Scottsdale. She couldn't begin to imagine what he would be doing in a family-owned liquor store in the southern end of Phoenix.

He grinned at her happily. "Mom had a doctor's appointment. Her arthritis, you know. It's a new guy she was recommended to. Anyway, I thought I'd stop in here and pick up something for dinner while I waited for her. Running into you is a nice bonus."

Devon's smile became genuine, but now she had to hold it back. She had been right. Where Russ went, Mom was sure to be close by.

"Really," he went on, "this is just a stroke of luck. I've been meaning to call you, but you're not listed in the phone book."

"Yes, I am. I'm in the yellow pages under Catering," she answered, then bit her tongue too late. He'd probably take the news as encouragement to call. Overload, she thought. The old brain's definitely on overload.

"Well, it doesn't matter. I can ask you now."

"Ask me what?" She continued to smile at him politely, but her eyes were wary. Her heart started sliding down toward her toes.

"To have dinner with me," he announced.

"Oh, Russ, I'm sorry, but this is a really bad week. I have—"

He laughed merrily, and her heart hit her toes with a thud. "No problem. I was thinking of next month. Seriously. I know how busy you are, so I thought I'd give us both a break by asking you early."

"It must be something in the water," she muttered to herself. Had chivalry returned, or was it her? She was beginning to think she'd give anything for a date within the week. She turned her attention back to Russ. "Next month?" she echoed disbelievingly.

"There's a fundraiser for Callahan on the twelfth. Has anyone invited you yet?"

I've probably had more invitations than Callahan himself, she thought grimly. She should have known that was what he had in mind, but the mention of Callahan still knocked the breath out of her. She struggled to keep her voice casual. "Actually," she answered, "I have about five hundred invitations."

Russ blinked at her. "Pardon me?"

"I'm catering it."

"Catering it? But I thought it was being held at the Diplomat Hotel."

"It is. The management donated the facilities but balked at throwing in their staff and supplying the meal. That's where I come in. So you see," she finished, pausing to give him what she hoped was a regretful smile, "I'll be seeing you there, but I wouldn't make the best date."

He looked so nonplussed she couldn't help feeling sorry for him. "Surely you'll find a minute or two to have a drink with me?" he tried again.

"Russ, I—" She broke off suddenly. An idea was germinating in the back of her brain. She shook her head to get rid of it. It was despicable, wrong.

It would buy her more time.

No. She couldn't do it. She shook her head again and looked up to meet Russ's confused eyes. "Of course I'll have a drink with you, if I can find the time. I can't promise anything though. We'll have to play it by ear. I'll see you there, okay? Right now I've got to run." She smiled at him weakly and started for the door again, her heart thudding sickly. The idea kept badgering her. She had to get out of there before she succumbed to the perfect temptation of it.

"Devon, wait!" Russ's voice stopped her as she stepped out onto the street. He pushed through the door after her. "Look, I've got an extra ticket. It's yours if you'll just take it. I know you're going to be busy with the catering, but whenever you can take a break, you'll have a seat to sit in."

Her heart started hammering. Her idea. It sounded even more horrible coming from his lips, but it sent her thoughts whirling busily. Showing up as Russ's date would offer her a perfect cover. She'd be able to take care of things in the kitchen and put on the appearance of being a paying guest as well.

Clay would be there, but he'd never have to know she was catering the affair. There would be five hundred people there. Even if he wanted to, he'd never be able to keep track of her all night.

It was perfect, but it was wrong. It would be her worst charade yet. It would be unfair to Russ. She forced herself to shake her head. "Russ, I know those are five-hundred-dollar tickets. I'm working the thing, remember? I'm not going to let you waste one on me."

"It wouldn't be a waste!" he protested.

"Yes, it would," she corrected him gently.

His jaw set stubbornly. "So what? It's my five hundred dollars. If I want to spend it for a few minutes with you as opposed to a whole evening with someone else, that's my prerogative."

She forced herself to meet his eyes honestly. "That's not the point, Russ," she answered softly. "That's not why you would be wasting it."

He flushed, and she felt like a heel. "I'm sorry," she hurried on. "I like you, Russ, but there's just nothing romantic about it. Please. Spend the money on someone else. There are probably a hundred women who would give their eyeteeth to spend some time with you." She wasn't sure it was true, but it sounded good. And God knew she didn't want to hurt him. She agreed with Moira. He was a genuinely nice guy.

Too nice. It would be too easy to use him. She turned on her heel again and started to cross the street toward her apartment.

"Please, Devon. I understand what you're saying, but I want you to go with me. I won't read anything into it."

She closed her eyes at the sound of his voice and stepped slowly up onto the curb again to avoid the onrush of traffic. What a weak, spineless creature she was, she thought disgustedly. Anything to salvage a relationship. Hadn't she learned the first time? She turned back to Russ with imploring eyes.

"Don't," she answered, shaking her head. "Please, Russ, don't push it." I'll give in, she thought wildly. And I can't do that. I can't do it to Clay and I can't do it to Russ.

But would she be using Russ if he understood where he stood with her? And how despicable could it be to buy just a little more time with Clay? After all the games she had played with him so far, what was one more? And the bottom line was that he had gone to that party the day before with someone else. Their relationship wasn't even an exclusive one. She *needed* more time.

And she knew suddenly that she was going to get it any way she could.

She laughed weakly. "It'll probably be the first time in history that a caterer is her own guest."

"Does that mean you'll come with me?"

"I—okay. But, Russ . . ." She trailed off, wanting to reiterate how she felt about him but not wanting to hurt him.

He spared her the necessity of it. Nodding, he answered, "I know," then added, "It starts at seven. Shall I pick you up at six? Of course, I'll give you a call before then, but—"

Devon shook her head. "It can't be that way. I'm going to have to be there hours early. I'll just have to meet you there."

Russ smiled. "If that's the way it has to be. Look, maybe afterward—"

"We'll see," she cut him off. "Listen, I really have to go now. I have a party to do tonight. I'll talk to you soon." She dredged up her best smile and started across the street again.

Her guilt dogged her footsteps mercilessly as she trotted up the steps to her second-floor apartment. It was a solution, she reminded herself, a perfect one. She wouldn't have to worry about telling Clay the truth before the twelfth. She'd been saved by a chance meeting in a liquor store.

But she didn't feel saved. She felt disgusted with herself.

She set the bags of liquor on the counter in the kitchen, then went back to the living room and dropped down onto the sofa. She massaged her temples, trying to ease the tension from her nerves. It was useless. That tension had been a permanent part of her for weeks now.

Maybe she should have told Russ the reason she had accepted the invitation. Maybe she should have told him about Clay. She still could. She could call him. Oh, hell, the damned fundraiser was next month. She had plenty of time, she had—

Her thoughts scattered as the jangling of the telephone intruded on the silence in the room. Devon jumped, her nerves feeling brittle and on the verge of disintegrating. Wearily, she got up to answer the call before the machine could do it for her.

"Hello?" She leaned back against the wall with a tired sigh. If it was another creditor, she swore she was simply going to hang up. Let them sue her. She couldn't take it anymore.

"Did I wake you? Being a lady of leisure is one thing, but it's two o'clock in the afternoon."

Clay. Her pulse leaped into a frantic pace despite the lethargy that had claimed her just moments before. She stood up straight. "Leisure? You've got to be kidding. I haven't stopped moving all day." That much was true, at least. How easy it would be to go on and tell him that she had spent the afternoon pleading with the owner of a liquor store for credit.

"I can believe that. You sound dead."

I am, she answered silently. Dead, and sick and tired of playing these games. I can't take it any more. Instead, she answered, "Actually, I do feel pretty dead. Someone should probably check me for vital signs."

Clay chuckled softly on the other end of the line. "I'd be happy to volunteer for the job."

"Something tells me you wouldn't get the job completed."

"Something tells me you're right." He paused, and his voice changed texture, becoming more like dark velvet. It made her knees feel weak. His impact on her never ceased to amaze her. The things she would do to hold on to him frightened her. She sat down slowly in the kitchen chair as he went on.

"Devon, I want to see you again. Soon."

She took a deep, steadying breath. "Before the twelfth of next month?"

"I was thinking of tomorrow night."

Did that mean he had plans with someone else tonight? Oh, God, she had to stop this. By his own admission and that of others, he was a loner. He socialized only when he had to. But he wanted to see her again; that had to mean something.

She nodded, then realized he couldn't see her. Yes, her brain was on overload. "I . . . sure, tomorrow's fine. I'm free."

"Good. I meant it when I said that I wanted you to come over for dinner. Shall I pick you up at seven?"

"Sure." Oh, God, what was she doing? Being tired of the games was one thing, but without them she had nothing. "No," she corrected herself quickly.

"Don't tell me. You've got plans and you're going to have to just show up again." The velvet disappeared from his voice. It sounded like steel. Devon shivered, but she knew that there was nothing she could do about it.

"Well . . . yes," she answered. "I'm sorry. I keep trying to tell you that I'm not the lady of leisure you envision."

There was a long pause. She sensed that she wasn't going to like his response, and the sound of her thundering heart seemed to fill the silence.

"I've wondered about that," he said eventually. "What do you do with your time? You've never told me."

The tension in her exploded and started to transform itself into a blinding headache. "I guess you could say I socialize a lot," she managed to answer. It was so close to being the truth, and so emphatically a lie. She grimaced. "Tell you what. Just give me your address and I'll be there at seven," she went on, trying to change the subject.

Clay finally acquiesced. She jotted down his address, managed to keep her voice light as she said good-bye, then went to dig out her precious bottle of bourbon. Her hands shook as she carefully measured out an ounce and mixed it with water. She watched them tremble, realizing that she was no longer surprised.

For someone who had displayed nerves of steel during the longest, most difficult year of her life, she was beginning to look like hell, Devon decided. She stared at her reflection in the full-length mirror on the back of her bedroom door. She'd have to do. She didn't have time to change again. It was ten after six, and it would take her at least half an hour to drive to Clay's house. What was more, there was still the issue of what she was going to do with her car once she got to Tatum Canyon. She didn't want Clay to see it. Ladies of leisure didn't drive around in Volkswagon Rabbits any more than they lived in three-room apartments in poor neighborhoods.

But that was another problem, and she still had at least half an hour to solve it. Her most immediate concern was the way she looked. Pleated white slacks camouflaged the ten pounds she had been walking around without for three weeks. Her bright blue silk blouse caught the color of her eyes and added a little vibrancy to her appearance. But nothing, not even twenty minutes of painstakingly applied makeup, could cover the dark smudges beneath her eyes. She chuckled humorlessly. She had bought herself more time, all right. The question was whether or not it was going to kill her.

She turned away from the mirror and plucked a lightweight jacket from the coat rack near the door. She slung it over her shoulder and trotted down the steps to the parking lot, her mind already moving on tirelessly to her second problem. What was she going to do with her car? And if she managed to hide it, how was she going to explain its absence?

She still hadn't come to a conclusion by the time she turned off Tatum Boulevard and headed up into the hills that cradled one of the most elite neighborhoods in the valley. Her thoughts picked at and fretted with the problem. Actually, concealing the car was the easy part, she decided, pulling up in front of a house that should, according to her calculations, be right around the corner from Clay's. The way her luck had been running, she even dared to hope that it would still be there when she came back for it, that the anonymous owners of the house wouldn't have it towed away. She got out of the car and glanced around the neighborhood. Hers was the only car visible. All the others were safely tucked away in garages. It *did* stick out like a sore thumb, but what else could she do? Her only choice was to hope that her luck would continue to hold the way it had for the last month. If Russ Sumner could suddenly turn up in a liquor store in the southern end of Phoenix, couldn't the owners of the house overlook a conspicuous Rabbit sitting in their front yard?

She left the car and started walking up the street. Turning the corner, she suddenly knew which house was Clay's without even looking at the address. All the homes were beautiful, but this one stood apart somehow, like the man himself. It was older, more classic. It sat perched on the side of the hill like a proud dowager overlooking her kingdom. Devon sighed and forced herself to walk up to the front door. Even as the weeks wore on, she never stopped feeling like a fraud.

She'd more or less gambled on the fact that a servant would answer the door, that she'd be able to slip inside without Clay noticing that her car was nowhere in sight. For once, her luck faltered.

The door swung open, and his partial smile greeted

her. His kiss was perfunctory, his eyes confused. They scanned the driveway and street quickly before coming back to her.

"I didn't hear you drive up. You didn't drive up." He paused, looking perplexed. "Did you?"

Devon opened her mouth without any idea of what was going to come out. "*I* didn't," she answered so smoothly that she startled even herself. "I had a friend drop me off."

Clay gave her another of his assessing looks as he ushered her inside. "Why?"

"Moira has my car," she answered nonchalantly. The lie was relatively easy to tell; it was so close to the truth. "Her Jaguar's in the shop. Someone backed into it and shattered a headlight. She has a busy week, so I gave her mine for the duration."

Clay took her jacket in the foyer and stared at her uncertainly. "And now you're spending the week hitching rides? Altruistic, aren't you?"

Devon shrugged helplessly. Her excuses were running dry.

"Well, I don't suppose it matters," he went on. "Come on in and get comfortable. I'll make you a drink."

"Bourbon and—" she began automatically, following him into the house.

"And water. I know. I remember." He smiled back at her as he glanced over his shoulder.

She followed him into the living room, biting her tongue against commenting on how many other women's drinks he'd been forced to memorize. It didn't matter, she reminded herself. She had bought time, and all good things took time. She started to smile at him as she joined him at the bar, feeling better than she had in days. Then, for the first time, the room hit her with its full impact.

"My God," she breathed, her eyes lifting to the twelve-foot-high ceiling, then dropping to scan the enormous room. "You could host the Callahan fundraiser right here."

"Not quite," he answered, but she hardly heard him as she pivoted slowly from her position at the bar. The room was vast, but more than that, it was beautiful. Oriental area rugs complimented the white tile floor. The fireplace was a single panel of blue-pearl granite that matched the bar and table tops. The furniture was contemporary and scant, clustered against the far wall, a solid expanse of glass beyond which twinkled a thousand city lights that looked like diamonds.

"Besides," he went on, and this time she turned to face him, "my flesh crawls at the idea of five hundred people converging on my home. I've never had more than ten people here at a time, and that was for Christmas dinner last year."

"Don't you ever get lonely?" she asked abruptly, accepting her drink from him. "I mean, there's so much house and so little you."

"I prefer it that way." He stirred his drink and left the bar to wander over to the windows. "I never get lonely."

Devon followed him and stepped up to his side. "I find that difficult to believe."

Suddenly he chuckled. "With good cause. I'm not so sure it's true."

She looked up at him, startled.

"It's sort of a blanket statement," he went on. "One I've been using for years without really thinking about it. It used to be true enough, but for the first time, right now, I really stopped to think about what I was saying and I saw holes in it."

"How so?"

He shrugged thoughtfully. "For years I had a fixation on big houses, big hotels. The roomier, the better. I guess I was trying to prove to myself that those early years in Chicago, those years I spent cramped up in three tiny rooms, were really behind me."

"And now?" she prodded him. She watched, fascinated, as a tiny muscle began to work in his jaw. He was unfolding right before her eyes again.

He was silent for a long minute before he answered.

"And now," he continued eventually, "now I stand here some nights with all this space around me and I feel alone. I look down on all those lights and I wonder where you are."

A tiny shiver slid down her spine. She suddenly felt dizzy, as though she were drowning in a maelstrom of conflicting emotions. Moments like these made it excruciating to remember that he was still seeing other women. Yet something warm and glowing and ecstatic flowed through her. She stared up at him speechless, wondering whether her heart was showing in her eyes.

Then, like the jungle cat she had thought of so often during their weekend in Denver, he retreated again. "Anyway," he said abruptly, "speaking of the Callahan fundraiser, have you come up with an answer for me yet?" He moved away from the window to freshen his drink and seemed to avoid looking at her.

Devon blanched. She followed him to the bar and pushed her drink at him for a refill. She was trembling again. It was time for another lie . . . her worst yet, in many ways. She felt as though the sun had set on her. One minute she had felt bright and alive. Now, in the next, she felt dull and depressed.

"I, uh . . . I can't go with you," she ground out from between clenched teeth. Then she immediately chastised herself. She had to do better than that. She had to make this lie sound convincing.

She looked up at Clay to find that his mouth had taken on an unpleasant twist. "How did I know that that was going to be the case?" he asked sarcastically, then added, "And why am I so damned disappointed?" He paused to search her face. "You're sure?"

Devon nodded dully. "I'm sorry. I really am. I would have loved to have gone with you."

"But?"

"But I agreed weeks ago to attend the affair with someone else."

The look he turned on her was more disbelieving than any she had seen yet. Her pulse started hammering as she watched him cross to the sofa near the window and sink down on it, shaking his head. "And you're just remembering this now?"

She followed him slowly and perched on the edge of the sofa beside him, clutching her drink. She swallowed hard as though that would help her force out the words. "I . . . I know. I can't believe I could be so forgetful. I was as surprised as you are when I checked my calendar."

"I don't believe this."

Devon felt her heart lurch. Did he mean that literally, or was it just a figure of speech? She couldn't tell. His expression was tight and his green-crystal eyes glittered, but with what she couldn't be sure. She spoke his name tentatively. "Clay?"

He slammed his glass down so hard on the cocktail table that she thought surely it would shatter. She jumped.

"I don't like this. I don't like this at all." He twisted to face her, and the expression in his eyes made her cringe. "Tell him you can't go with him."

Devon gaped at him and breathed the first thing that came to her mind. "I can't do that. They're five-hundred-dollar tickets."

"As you're so fond of telling me, the damned thing is a month away. He'll find someone else."

It was a plausible argument. Her thoughts whirled as she tried to think of some way to refute it. She couldn't, and what was worse, she was so tired, so very tired, of lying like this. A soft moan slid from her as she jumped to her feet. It had been such a great plan she thought, staring out the window. But she hadn't considered all eventualities. And now one was trapping her.

She was distantly aware of him moving behind her. She could hear him pacing, then dropping more ice cubes into his glass at the bar. When his voice finally came again, she jumped.

"I've made a decision," he said suddenly. She pivoted to face him. He stood behind the bar, both hands outstretched and braced on it. His mouth was thin with thought, but he looked more relaxed than he had since their conversation started.

"Regarding what?" she managed.

"I don't want to share you. Not with the ghost of your ex-husband and not with this character you're supposed to go to the fundraiser with. It's something that's been creeping up on me for awhile. The other day at the zoo . . ." He trailed off and shook his head, then took a fortifying swallow of his drink. The smile he turned on her was oddly resigned. "Well, you know how I reacted to that conversation. Can you believe me when I tell you that no one was more surprised than I was?"

Devon nodded slowly, silently. She stared at him as the first warmth of hope slid through her.

"And then, that afternoon at the Carlsons' party . . . all I could think about was you. Something's happening to me, Devon. You're doing something to me, changing me. I'm not happy alone anymore. Hell, I'm not all that happy with my *life* anymore. I've been trying to ignore it, but now you stand there and tell me point blank that you have a date with someone else, and—" He paused again and shook his head. "And every bone in my body fights back at the thought. Don't do it, Devon. I don't want to share you."

He downed the last of his drink and came around the bar toward her. When his hands found her shoulders and the warmth of him radiated through her, she thought she would faint. Her heart hammered in panic; her knees felt weak with joy.

"Cancel it. Don't go with him," he murmured in a husky voice. "God help me, I don't want you to see anyone else."

Her panic rose. It tore her breath away and a short gasp escaped her. She pulled away from him, feeling her trembling reach the deepest part of her soul.

She was trapped. She was trapped as she had never been before.

She couldn't meet his eyes. Every part of her longed to agree with him, to tell him that she had no desire to date anyone else either. She wanted to tell him that she wouldn't go with Russ to the fundraiser, but she couldn't. Because if she didn't go with Russ, she would have to tell Clay the truth.

Her response came out strangled and harsh. In fighting her predicament, she could only end up fighting him. "You don't want to share me," she snapped, "but I'm supposed to keep my mouth shut while you gallivant around town with God knows how many other women. I keep telling you that you have a lot to learn about the equality of the sexes, Clay. Your first lesson ought to be that what's good for the goose is good for the gander."

He looked at her blankly. "What?"

"You were the one to set the ground rules here. You've never rubbed my nose in it, but it's been pretty obvious that you've been dating other women. Like Monday night's anniversary bash, for instance. Now you decide that you don't want to share me, and that's just fine, but I've got a date on the twelfth."

She turned back to face him, every muscle in her body quivering. She more than expected to be faced with the same stony anger she had seen in his eyes when she had tried to tell him about Ian. Instead his expression was soft, even gentle.

"I'm sorry," he said simply. "We were well beyond the point of dating other people when I went to that anniversary party the other day. I knew that and I went anyway . . . and yes, I did take someone else. My only excuse is that I was trying to escape what was happening between us. Now I'm beginning to think that there's no escape to be had."

Confusion assailed her. She moved slowly to the sofa on legs that felt amazingly weak and sank down on it again. A frustrated, almost inaudible cry escaped her. She had waited and waited for the right time to tell him the truth . . . and now it seemed as though it had passed right by without her even noticing it. Two days before, he had still been dating other women. Now he wanted her all to himself.

And now she had already told him the lie about Russ.

Was it possible to back out of it again? Could she tell him that she had lied because she didn't want him to know she was catering the party? No, God no. That was worse than simply telling him the truth . . . and that would be hard enough. She looked up at him with an imploring gaze, her heart aching with frustration.

He reached out and brushed a curl of hair from her forehead so tenderly that she wanted to sob. The uncertainty in his eyes was almost more than she could bear. What was she doing to him?

"Hey, what I'm saying isn't that bad, is it?" he asked softly.

She shook her head numbly as he sat down beside her.

"Devon, try to understand. I've spent every single moment of the years since my divorce actively trying not to get involved with anyone. My methods were numerous." He paused to smile at her sourly. "I scheduled dates months in advance and for specific affairs. That way no one woman could believe that I wanted to see only her. It always appeared as though I needed a date. And I constantly rotated the few women I went out with. I spent the weekend with you, so I took someone else to the Carlsons' party. It was habit, but I realized that afternoon that it was also useless." He chuckled softly, and this time his accompanying smile was more genuine. "The whole time I was with . . . this other woman . . . at the Carlsons', I thought of you. I kept visualizing you there, imagining the things you would say, how you would act with such boring, stodgy people. I wondered how they would take to your bluntness. And I suddenly knew that the only person in the world I wanted to be there with was you."

Devon laughed weakly. "That's a hell of a way to be remembered."

"The point is, for the first time in years, I don't want to date anyone else. I'm not afraid of getting involved, not with you. I *want* to be involved with you." Suddenly he

135

jumped to his feet. Devon's nerves were so wired that she flinched. "God!" he murmured vehemently. "I can't believe I'm saying this!"

He turned away from the window again to look down at her. "Devon, I really don't want to get married again. I no longer believe in the institution, and I have no desire to tangle with it."

Devon stared up at him, her heart in her throat. "What . . . what are you saying?" she breathed.

He took a deep breath, as though he was trying to brace himself against his own words. "I don't want to get married, but I want you to move in with me. Here. Now."

The shock of his statement hit her full force. She stared at him, tongue-tied, her emotions so chaotic that confusion crashed against her in waves. She opened her mouth to speak, then clamped her lips shut again. An indecipherable moan sounded deep in the back of her throat.

Nothing could have stunned her more than his proposal. Nothing . . . except the extent to which she wanted to say yes.

Longing, pure and powerful, rocked through her. Yes, she wanted to live with him. Yes, she wanted to be a part of his world. Hadn't she wanted that from the first time she had laid eyes on him? And now, so many months later, that desire was a pulsing, undeniable part of her. She continued to stare at him, speechless with the agony of wanting to say yes.

"Damn it!" he growled. "Talk to me. Say something. This isn't something I'm in the habit of doing every day of the week."

Her breath came out in a sharp gasp. Yes, she had to say something. She had to tell him the truth. Now.

It was time.

"I . . . I'll give you my answer in a minute . . . if you still want me to." It occurred to her that these were the hardest words she'd ever had to speak; then she thought of what still lay ahead. She stood up shakily, then closed her eyes. "I've got to tell you something first," she whispered.

She opened her eyes again to find that a dark cloud had settled over his. "Does this have anything to do with what we started to discuss the other day?"

She forced herself to nod.

"Then don't. Not now. Not ever. Just be mine."

He pulled her almost violently to him. She came up against his chest with an impact that almost took her breath away. She opened her mouth to try to tell him one last time, but then he was touching her again. Her words dissolved on her tongue. They fell forgotten to the back of her brain. Nothing mattered but the feel of him; nothing was as important as his touch.

Her arms encircled his neck as she buried her face against his throat, breathing in the faint aroma of his aftershave, that elusive but distinct scent that had once reminded her so much of his personality. Then his hand found her chin and tilted her face upward so that his mouth could claim hers. His fingers slid into her hair and his free hand pressed into the small of her back as he kissed her. His strength was the only thing that kept her on her feet as he held her against him. His kisses were intoxicating, powerful enough to drive even the most tormenting demons from her mind.

His tongue sent surges of need through her as it slid over her teeth and traced her lips. She trembled with feverish urgency as she buried her hands in his hair and pressed her mouth against his. Suddenly nothing was as important as the moment, as sharing just one more electric hour with him. It might be the last time she'd ever touch him, but it might be the beginning of a thousand new hours too. The thought ignited her, and she kissed him back fervently. Either way, this was going to be a night to remember.

His lips were hard and searching as he eased her down onto the sofa again. Devon held his mouth with her own as a hunger that startled even her roared through her. Her fingers trembled as they worked at the buttons of his shirt. When they were finally free, she pushed the fabric aside impatiently. His chest was lean and sinewy, but so smooth. She ran her palms over his skin, savoring the feel of him. He was the most perfect man in the world and, for the moment at least, he was hers.

The satiny caress of her hands seemed to be Clay's undoing. If before she had sensed the finest thread of restraint in him, now it threatened to snap. He groaned and buried his face against her neck as his fingers went to the buttons of her blouse. When they didn't pop free easily, he pulled at them harder until the last two snapped free, bounding down onto the oriental rug. Devon was too drugged with the desire pounding in her to care. She shrugged out of the silk and reached out for him again, clutching him to her. Instinctively, she arched upward, wanting to feel as much of him as she could. She had to feel his flesh against hers, wanted nothing more than to meld with him finally and completely.

Their legs became entangled. Devon moved one of her legs on top of his and groaned quietly as his thigh came up between hers. He moved it slowly and deliberately as his lips bore down on the soft skin of her breasts. She could no longer think of sensations separately, but drowned under the assault of all of them as his tongue teased her nipple. His name formed a desperate plea upon her lips.

It was enough to shatter the last of his restraint. She wasn't disappointed. She needed more of him than what he was giving her. She cried out softly as he shifted slightly above her, his mouth trailing down over her ribs to her stomach. It seemed as though hours passed before his lips found the barrier of her slacks. Devon floated on a cloud of endless suspense, her whole being poised in waiting. Finally, when she could hold her breath no longer, his fingers found the snap and zipper of her slacks. His hand slid beneath them, over her taut stomach to the swell of her hips. As he slid her slacks down over her legs, he bent over her again. His tongue found her navel, then inched gradually lower as he moved her slacks down over her thighs.

He was taking such time, such care. The waiting seemed interminable before she finally felt his mouth against her thigh. She moaned and moved unconsciously against him until she felt the light friction of his tongue again. This time it caught the center of her yearning and brought a flood of heat swirling through her body.

She gasped as it seared through her. The sound seemed to ignite Clay as well, and the passion between them became all-encompassing. He straightened and loomed over her, parting her thighs with his knee again. The movement wasn't gentle. It was aggressive and very nearly desperate. As he filled her, she cried out again, but this time it was a sound of release and satisfaction. His eyes caught hers as he moved within her. The need inside her began to writhe toward explosion and she looked away, but his hand came up to bring her face around to his again. With his eyes locked on hers, he pushed into her. She answered his desperation with her own, locking her legs around him, holding him to her as the heaviness of her desire for him erupted and crashed through her.

She almost didn't hear him. Her own emotions were a deafening roar in her ears, nearly obliterating all else. But somehow his voice managed to penetrate as he shuddered slightly and stiffened above her.

"Oh, God, Devon, I love you."

Her tears came suddenly, quietly. A single, tortured sob caught in her throat as she twisted her face away to stare out at the glimmering city lights beneath them. One solitary, hot tear slid down her cheek, leaving a desolate spot on the upholstery. How easy it would be to put words to the delicate, quivering emotion that hovered on her lips, shocking even her.

She loved him too.

10

~~~~~~~~

Her pulse was a throbbing headache at her temples.
Devon threw her head back and forced herself to swallow
two more aspirins. They had to work this time. This same
headache had been dogging her for weeks, but that night
it simply had to go. That night she *had* to think clearly;
she had to be on her toes. That night was the grand finale
of her charade.

She left the bathroom, flipping the light switch off
behind her. Actually, she had been thinking of the
fundraiser in terms of a grand finale all week. She had
gotten it into her head that it was a culmination of sorts. If
she could just get through this night, if she could just get
through Callahan's fundraiser, everything would be fine.

It wasn't a wholly unrealistic fantasy, she thought,
going back to the bedroom to finish dressing. The check
she would receive from Bill Murdock that night would be
large enough to allow her to start whittling away at her
debts. And approximately five hundred of the "right"
people would be there to eat her food and sample her

hospitality, giving her a chance to prove herself. Of course, it would mean swallowing her pride as she had never done before. And it meant taking a risk that was almost unbearable in its potential danger. But in those respects too, it was a new beginning.

The fundraiser would mark the first time in nearly fifteen months that she would face virtually all of her old "friends" at the same time. A few of them had been at the Myers' cocktail party two months earlier, but she knew that a gala affair like Callahan's fundraiser would bring them out in droves. She closed her eyes briefly, her shoulders sagging as she paused for a moment before putting the finishing touches on her makeup. Could she do it? Could she face them?

Who was she kidding? She had no choice.

She forced herself to look at the bright side. Most of the guests would, like Clay, fall victim to the charade she was putting on. With any luck, they would believe she was a paying guest until the whole thing was over. Of course, her presence would raise a few eyebrows. She doubted if there was anyone who didn't know what Ian had done to her, and her appearance would invite speculation.

Just please, God, don't let anyone speculate in front of Clay, she prayed. She could handle their haughty looks. She would choke back her pride and face them all down. Just so long as she got through the evening without Clay learning the truth from someone else.

Panic began to flutter within her as she realized what a long shot that would be. All it would take was one person with a big mouth, one person hell-bent on embarrassing her. They had never liked her before—she had been too blunt for their refined tastes—and it was ludicrous to assume that they would like her any more now. They would think nothing of rehashing her misfortune within the hearing of anyone who cared to listen. Including Clay.

She shivered slightly. The odds were stacked against her, and she had no choice but to take the gamble.

She stepped back from the mirror to examine her reflection more fully, but her scrutiny stopped when she met her own eyes. "This is the last time," she promised herself. "This is positively the last time."

It was a vow she'd made to herself weeks before. She'd play no more games with Clay after this night. She knew she couldn't continue with her cloak-and-dagger routine much longer. She couldn't take it anymore. Tension had been building slowly and insidiously within her over the course of the past month. She felt as though she were on the verge of exploding. She'd lost five more pounds. Her appetite had vanished, and she wasn't sleeping well. And *that* was a sign of stress difficult to camouflage; she'd been spending almost every other night at Clay's.

She hadn't tried to tell him the truth again, not after the first night at his house when he had asked her to move in with him. Neither had she given him a definitive answer regarding his proposal. The words had been on her lips a thousand times, but she hadn't given them voice. She couldn't. She couldn't move in with him until she told him the truth, and she couldn't tell him the truth until her scheme with Russ and the fundraiser was behind her. With any luck, she would be able to come clean with him then without citing all the details of her various lies. With any luck, those lies would pass by without mention, like water under a bridge.

She scowled at her reflection and adjusted the straps of the pale blue satin dress she had borrowed from Moira. She knew she was stalling, but she was scared. She was dressing for so much more than appearances with Clay. She was dressing for five hundred people who could ruin everything for her. But she was doing it in style. Moira had lent her a pair of diamond and sapphire earrings too, and she pushed them through her pierced ears, securing them carefully. Then she fastened the matching teardrop choker around her neck, reached for her purse, and stoically walked toward the door.

Her determination felt like a rock in her throat. She

felt sure she would choke on it before the night was out.

"Are you sure you're okay?" She met Lisa Cheney's eyes doubtfully as they stood in the corridor outside the kitchen of the Diplomat Hotel. One end of the corridor opened onto the lobby of the hotel. The other opened onto the banquet room. Devon struggled to keep her eyes from roaming in that direction to look for Clay.

Her assistant nodded at her. "I think so. But you'll come back and check in with me once in awhile?"

Devon nodded emphatically. "Of course. This is the night I've been waiting for for a year. You don't think I'm going to let anything fall to chance, do you?"

Lisa met her eyes candidly. "To tell you the truth, I don't know. You've been acting so odd lately. I can't believe that after all this time we finally get a party of this magnitude, and you're going to abandon Gayle and me and go sit out front."

Devon's smile faded. "I have no choice," she reminded her. "This night is more important to me than you'll ever know. And a lot of it hinges on me being out front."

Lisa sighed. "I'm sorry. I'm just scared. We've never done anything this big. I—"

Gayle Clement suddenly stuck her head out of the kitchen. "If you'll just stop whimpering about it and get a move on, everything will be fine," she called out to the other woman. Then she caught Devon's eyes. "Don't worry. We're okay. For heaven's sake, you put the entire meal together. We're perfectly capable of getting it on the tables."

Devon gave her a grateful smile. It was true, really. Not much could go wrong now. The temporaries she had hired to help serve were all present and accounted for. They had all been briefed and knew what they were doing, from the waiters clear on down to the bartender. She had spent the entire week cooking and freezing and planning. Everything was fine.

With one minor exception. Her stomach felt like the inside of a pressure cooker.

She pressed her hand to her waist instinctively as she turned to head down the hallway. Then she caught herself and changed direction. It wouldn't do to be seen coming from the kitchen. She had been making all her visits to Gayle and Lisa the long way, circling through the lobby to leave and enter through the main doors of the banquet room. Now was not the time to get sloppy. Too many people were beginning to arrive.

Russ, of course, had been among the first. He'd caught up to her in the kitchen forty minutes earlier, and it had been the first and only time she had allowed her panic to make her lose her cool. She'd grabbed his arm unthinkingly and steered him back to the dining room via the lobby. Only when they were safely seated again had her panic cleared enough to enable her to tell him that she didn't want anyone to know she was the caterer. He'd thought he understood. He knew the trouncing her pride had taken in the past year. What he didn't know was that she'd gladly throw her pride out the window to ensure that Clay Wyatt didn't learn what was going on.

Now, as she reached the dining room again, she allowed her eyes to scan the crowd that was beginning to accumulate. She tried to tell herself she was looking for Russ, but her gaze searched for tawny hair sprinkled with gray, for aloof green eyes that subtly mocked the group around him. She didn't find either. Clay wasn't there yet. She let out a small sigh and concentrated more fully on locating Russ.

"There you are. How's it going? You know, that dress looks better on you than it does on me. Maybe I should have a wild, stressful affair and lose fifteen pounds. Marital bliss is killing my waistline."

Devon whirled around to find Moira standing at her elbow. "Will you hush?" she whispered. "I don't want anyone to know that I borrowed all this stuff from you."

Moira's grimace was both contrite and sympathetic. "I

know. I'm sorry. I wasn't thinking. God, I admire you for doing this. I'm not sure I'd have the guts."

"Guts have nothing to do with it. Imminent starvation is more like it. Besides, the only people who know I'm the caterer are you and Derrick and Russ. For the time being, anyway. Later, I want them all to know that I put this stupendous meal together and hire me to do their next party. But in the meantime, let's hope that everyone just assumes that I've emerged from my cocoon of poverty."

"And doesn't comment on it," Moira muttered.

"Bingo."

Moira shrugged. "Well, I'll do all I can to keep tongues from wagging in front of the wrong people, such as a millionaire with green eyes."

Devon let out a helpless sigh. "Moira, we're talking five hundred tongues here. Even your talents won't stretch that far. I think I'm reduced to relying on luck tonight."

"Oh, Devon," Moira said, "If only you had come to more of my parties. Maybe this wouldn't be so much of a surprise to people. Your showing up here, I mean."

Devon laughed humorlessly. "Well, you know what they say. Hindsight is useless. I wish I had too, but I was too mortified at the time. Hell, I'm mortified now. Hunger pangs can make you do just about anything, I guess." She glanced around to give her friend a grateful look. "Your help has made all the difference, you know. Thanks again for all this." She tugged on an earring. "You haven't just saved my skin with Clay again. You've saved it with roughly two hundred and fifty bloodthirsty women as well."

Moira shrugged, looking a little embarrassed. "It's just a dress and a few pieces of jewelry."

"A few pieces of jewelry," Devon scoffed. "I'm walking around with half the United States Treasury hanging around my neck."

Moira shook her head. "It doesn't matter. You look great in it. By the way, speaking of Clay and our little ruses to keep him blissfully ignorant, how much longer is this going to go on?"

Devon continued to survey the people in the room. "Not long," she answered flatly, not looking at Moira.

"That was question number one. Question number two is why he asked me about my Jaguar."

Devon froze as her eyes flicked over the room. She slowly turned back to Moira. "He asked you about what?"

"About the broken headlight on my Jaguar." Moira's eyes narrowed as she took in Devon's stricken expression. "What does it mean?"

"It means," Devon responded hollowly, "that he's getting suspicious."

Icy fear twisted around her heart as she turned away from her friend and went to find Russ. She had to struggle for even fragile control as she spotted him at their table and slid into the chair beside him.

Clay was beginning to suspect something. The realization pounded at her brain until her headache threatened to become excruciating. Well, what had she expected? She had told him so many half-baked stories, had offered him so many questionable excuses. A five-year-old child would be growing doubtful by now. So he had checked one of her excuses with Moira. So what? He'd know the truth soon anyway. She reached for her water glass shakily and swallowed from it, trying to push down some of the panic that was welling in her throat.

"I was just beginning to wonder if you'd ever come back."

She looked at Russ with a weak smile. "Sorry, but you can't say I didn't warn you," she whispered.

He grinned at her warmly. "I'll take what I can get."

Come on, get into the act, she chastised herself. She forced herself to smile more widely. "What you get just might be an embarrassing temper tantrum. I'm not sure sitting out here is such a good idea. If I hear one person complain about the food, I'm liable to launch myself over the table at them and throttle them."

"Well, it might liven things up a bit. So far, the food's been the most exciting aspect of the night."

She squeezed his hand. "Thanks, but that doesn't say much for the public appeal of Callahan if an appetizer can upstage him."

Russ gave her an odd look. "He's not here yet."

Devon felt sick embarrassment slide over her. "Oh. I guess I was too tied up with the meal to notice."

"Well, you're the only one. Rumors are running rampant that he's too sick to attend. There's been so much speculation about his health. I—"

Russ broke off suddenly and looked up. Startled, Devon followed his eyes.

Clay stood beside their table. A soft yearning made her feel light-headed as she met his eyes. The two other couples seated at the table glanced up as well, but Clay's eyes never left hers to acknowledge them. His smile was small, almost infinitesimal, but she caught it. It was meant just for her.

Russ got to his feet and extended his hand. "Clay, it's good to see you again."

"Yes," Devon murmured, holding his eyes. "It is." She had left him at eight o'clock that morning. Looking at him again, it seemed like light-years ago. She forgot that he had questioned Moira about her Jaguar. She forgot everything but the smile on his lips and the intimate look in his eyes. Maybe he was becoming suspicious but, at the moment, his gaze was warm and uncomplicated. If he had any doubts about her excuses, they didn't show in his eyes now.

Then the glowing serenity in her heart shattered. He pulled out the chair across from her and sat down.

She choked back a startled cry. "You're . . . sitting here?"

"It took a bit of bribery, but yes." Suddenly his voice dropped to a husky undertone. "Geese and ganders be damned. I don't give up without a fight."

She sat back hard against her chair, feeling the room spin away from her. Everything—the success of the whole night—had depended on him not being able to keep tabs on her. The conversation buzzing around her suddenly seemed like a deafening roar as she felt herself sinking faster and faster into an uncontrollable panic.

"Devon?" It was Russ. His hand covered hers as he tried to get her attention. Clay noticed and his eyes darkened. This is impossible, she thought wildly. I can't do this!

"Callahan just arrived," Russ went on. He nodded toward the back of the room. Every head at the table turned except Clay's. His eyes were on hers, as intent as they had been the first night she had met him. She shivered and tried for a smile that fell horribly short.

"Didn't you . . . uh . . . want to see how he looked? Callahan, that is. We were talking about how sick he really is, remember?" Her voice was a tremulous whisper. Oh, God, she was going to ruin this!

"I talked to him out in the lobby. He looks just like any other seventy-two-year-old man. I'm more interested in looking at you."

She nodded and followed everyone's eyes toward the door. She tried to concentrate on Callahan as he made his way toward the dais, but Clay's gaze pulled at her, demanding her attention. She couldn't help herself. She sighed and turned back to him, then caught her breath.

Directly behind him, Lisa was beckoning to her from the door to the corridor.

Devon jumped to her feet. "I . . . excuse me. I've got to go to the ladies' room."

She pushed past Callahan's entourage and hurried out into the lobby. She cast a quick look around to make sure there was no one else in the area to notice her. The coast was clear. Thank God, she thought, the Senator had arrived when he had. With any luck, everyone's attention would be on him.

She caught up with Lisa in the corridor. "What is it?"

Lisa looked startled. "Oh. It's okay now. I got confused about which sauce went on the asparagus, but Gayle straightened me out."

Devon stared at her with a horrified look. "The

asparagus? You forgot which sauce went on the *asparagus*? You called me back here for that?"

Gayle whizzed by them on her way into the kitchen. "Take it easy on her. It's stage fright. I'll get her calmed down before the main course is over."

"By then it'll probably be too late," Devon murmured under her breath. She turned on her heel again and rushed back into the lobby. She thought she'd been prepared for anything, but she never considered that Lisa might fall apart under pressure. Yet there was no time to worry about it now. As she neared the banquet room again, fresh panic claimed her as she thought of what she had to return to.

It wasn't as bad as she feared. Callahan was speaking, and all eyes in the room were focused on him, including Clay's. He turned a smile on her as she sat down again, but the majority of his attention remained on the senator. Devon breathed a small sigh of relief and allowed her eyes to scan the room.

The temporaries she had hired were right on top of things. She thought again of Lisa and wished she had had the foresight to put her in the dining room and one of the extras in the kitchen. Oh, well, it was too late now. At least no one knew what was going on down the corridor. All the guests were aware of was the food, and that, thankfully, was being served without a hitch. She tried to overhear any comments her dinner partners might have about its quality.

Then her gaze fell on the door to the corridor again. Gayle hovered there, trying to catch her eye.

Devon's heart plummetted down into her toes. She squeezed her eyes shut briefly. If she jumped up again now, so soon after she had sat down and right in the middle of Callahan's speech, every eye in the place would be on her. She swallowed hard, trying to find the courage to force herself to do it. She had no choice.

She offered the people at the table an apologetic smile as she got to her feet. Clay's eyebrows rose as he fixed her with one of his speculative looks.

"I . . . uh, I haven't felt very well all day. I . . . excuse me again."

She didn't look back this time. If Gayle thought it prudent to get her into the kitchen, something might be seriously wrong. She walked as fast as she could through the lobby; then, as soon as she reached the opposite end of the corridor, she broke into a run.

Gayle and Lisa were both in the kitchen. Waiters hustled in and out, balancing huge trays on their shoulders. It was a madhouse, but at least it seemed like a controlled madhouse. Devon walked up to Gayle and tapped her on the shoulder.

"You wanted me?"

Gayle shrugged apologetically. "I'm sorry. Things seem to be approaching a panic point here. We're a little short-handed getting the main course out. It's not a problem yet, and I know it's important to you to stay out front tonight, but I also know that it's important that this fundraiser comes off without a hitch. I gambled on the fact that you'd want your extra pair of hands in here to nip the problem in the bud."

Devon sighed. "You gambled right." She grabbed an apron from a nearby rack and moved around behind the counter to pull the sole turbans from the oven and put them on plates. Gayle appeared at her side instantly.

"Let me do that. You garnish the plates before they go out. You won't be able to go back to your table if you get butter all over your dress."

Devon gave her a tight, grateful smile and changed places with her. Gayle's assessment of the situation had been entirely accurate. They hadn't reached the panic point yet, and with her extra hands they avoided it. Within twenty minutes, Gayle and Lisa were hoisting the last trays onto their shoulders to take them out to the waiters' stations.

Devon let out a shaky breath and reached behind her to untie her apron. She dropped it back on the rack again and smoothed it unthinkingly as she tried to steady her singing nerves. She glanced down at her watch. She had been gone for twenty-two minutes. It would be absurd to think that no one had noticed. Clay certainly would. Yet standing there trying to think of an excuse wasn't going to help. The longer she stayed away, the worse the dilemma became. She'd just have to go back and wing it. She bit her lip and turned for the door, then froze.

Clay stood there. She pressed her hand to her mouth to stifle her cry of shock.

He took another step into the room. "What's going on?" he asked, his voice too casual, the question too idle. Devon felt a thousand icy fingers begin to pluck at her skin.

"How . . . how long have you been standing there?" she managed to ask, then answered herself silently. Long enough. One corner of his mouth twisted downward forbiddingly. His eyes assessed her almost coldly.

"Long enough to watch you lend a helping hand to the kitchen crew," he answered. He ran his hand over the counter nonchalantly, then turned abruptly back to her. "Why?" he demanded.

She opened her mouth to answer, but he cut her off. "The truth this time, Devon."

She nodded miserably. At least it came as no surprise that he had become suspicious of her excuses, she thought wildly.

"Well?" he prodded her.

She took a deep, convulsive breath. "I was helping the kitchen crew because I am the kitchen crew. I'm the caterer."

It was out. Just three short words—"I'm the caterer"— and the entire impossible charade was over. Her heart thudded sickly as she forced herself to meet his eyes. The waiting seemed interminable as she watched for understanding to dawn there.

But his eyes didn't change. They remained enigmatic as he looked away from her to glance around the kitchen. Finally, he nodded thoughtfully. "This is what you do for

151

a living? This is the socializing you told me about?" he asked too calmly.

"I—yes," she answered cautiously.

Then he turned back to her with a smile that made her blood run cold. "I've got to hand it to you. You tell dandy lies. But that wasn't really a lie, was it? Just an . . . evasion. 'I guess you could say I socialize a lot,' " he mimicked her soft voice. "Isn't that what you told me when I asked you what you did with your days?"

Ice spread through the pit of her stomach. "I—" she began, but he cut her off again.

"Who is he?" he growled suddenly.

"Who?" she whispered.

"The jerk you're sitting next to out there. The one who's been staring at you with big puppy-dog eyes and grabbing your hand every thirty seconds."

Devon took a deep breath. This much she could handle. "You know who he is. You know Russ."

His expression became even more derisive. "Sure I do. What I don't know, what I'm asking you, is why you told me you had a date with him when in truth you were going to be catering this thing. Was it another . . . uh, *evasion?*"

She shook her head emphatically. "No! I *am* his date. I'm just the caterer too." Clay's eyes became stonier, and she rushed on. "He doesn't mean anything to me! I've never even gone out with him before. This is the first time I've ever done anything other than run into him somewhere. I—"

"That's reassuring. It's not, however, the answer I asked for," he interrupted. "Come to think of it, you've never been real long on answers. Phony ones, yes—but the truth? Damn it, Devon, you've been telling me lies! We've just uncovered two of them in five minutes! How many others are there?"

She swallowed convulsively again. "They weren't lies, just . . . just . . ."

He shot her a dark, disbelieving glance. "Just what?

Fibs? Fibs are for kids, Devon. After you grow up, you get to call them lies. They're one of the pitfalls of maturity. After you hit twenty-one, there's no easy way out of them anymore."

"Okay! Okay, so they were lies of omission!"

"Omission," he echoed. His laugh chilled her. He reached for her suddenly and pulled her toward him until she had no choice but to face the cold anger in his eyes. If she had any doubt that he wasn't as calm as he appeared, the pain of his fingers biting into her arm dispelled it.

"You and your omissions," he sneered. "You've given me enough of them, haven't you? You omitted telling me what you do for a living, you omitted telling me anything about your past until it was so late that I didn't want to hear it, you . . ." He trailed off and released her abruptly. Devon took a quick, unsteady step backward and rubbed her arm. He turned away from her and ran his hand through his hair. Nausea churned in her throat as she watched him with eyes wide with pain and disbelief. How could he be so unfair? He could remember that she had tried to tell him the truth, but he obviously didn't care to remember that he had cut her off. She would have hated him for his convenient memory if it hadn't been for the remorse that was choking her.

He chuckled humorlessly, bringing her attention back to him. "I swore I'd never be any woman's fool again. But I was as naïve and as trusting with you as I was with my mother the day I was born. You know, I used to think that it was exciting and refreshing to know so little about you," he went on, turning back to her. "And I trusted you enough to be able to live with it. But I had no business trusting you. You were lying to me, betraying that trust, every step of the way. I thought I was in love with you, but my God, I don't even know you! I've got enough facts about you to fit in the palm of my hand, and that's about it. And God only knows if those are true or not."

She closed her eyes. A raw, elemental pain flooded through her at the torment in his voice. Oh, God, what had she done to him?

He leaned closer to her and she jumped at the sound of his voice again, her eyes flying open. "Who are you, Devon Jordan? A pathological liar? A paranoid eccentric? Damn it, answer me! I don't even know where you live! Why?"

Suddenly, white-hot rage ripped through her, so strong and so instantaneous that it took her breath away. Yes, she had been wrong, but she had never meant to hurt him. She had tried to tell him the truth, even knowing that she would lose him. Yet he didn't remember that. He remembered only enough to make her seem like a cold, calculating bitch. Yet every lie she had told him had taken its toll of her in guilt and remorse and fear. She buckled suddenly under the weight of it all, reacting furiously to the contempt in his voice that she had dreaded from the beginning.

"You don't know anything about me because I spared you the trouble!" she screamed. "I kept you from making an idiot of yourself! If you can stand there and tell me that you would have attended this fundraiser with the hired help, then you're a bigger liar than I am! You want to know why I came here with Russ? Okay, I'll tell you. I came with Russ because he's not so damned stuck on his image that he'd mind being seen with me. I came with Russ because his overriding achievement in life hasn't been protecting his millions from women like me!"

A silent chill settled over the room as she finished. "Women like you?" Clay repeated eventually.

"Now you're catching on," she snapped. "Yes, women like me." Her blue eyes blazed and her fingers trembled with fury as she pulled Moira's choker from her neck and ripped her earrings from her ears. She threw them at him in frustrated rage. They hit his chest, then scattered to the floor.

Neither of them made any move to retrieve them. They both stood frozen as Devon stared at him, her chest heaving. "They're not mine," she finished, her voice dead and lifeless now. "I couldn't possibly afford them. Do you understand now? I cater parties like this chiefly for the privilege of putting food in my mouth." She paused to glare at him, her face dangerously pale, her eyes burning. "I do it for the luxury of paying the rent on a three-room apartment on McDowell Road. That's the new house you've never seen. So tell me, Clay, and remember—honesty's the name of the game now. Do you want me without the jewelry? Do you want me like this? Do you love what I'm telling you?" Her voice rose again, becoming almost hysterical. *"How the hell do you feel about me without all the trappings of the lifestyle that's so precious to you?"*

He seemed to move slightly, then hesitated. Devon's heart hurled itself into her throat as she waited for him to say something, to do something. Then he started backing toward the door.

It was no more or less than she had expected, but a bitter, cold despair welled up in her throat. The hope she had been nourishing for two months died. She couldn't bear to look at him. She bowed her head, her shoulders slumping as she leaned back against the wall weakly.

"Well, I guess that says it all," she whispered. "More clearly than words, actually. Go on, Clay. Get out of here. I have work to do."

She waited for the sound of movement, and when it didn't come, she forced herself to look up at him again. He stood in the doorway, both hands braced against the jambs. His eyes were fiery as they flicked over her, his voice empty.

"I think—I think I would have wanted you under any circumstances," he answered. "But I can't live with your lies, Devon. I don't care why you told them. You did it. That's the bottom line. I trusted you and you betrayed that trust. I don't even know who the hell you are, and I'll be damned if I'm going to share my life with a stranger. I don't care where you live, but it sure as hell isn't going to be with me."

His footsteps clicked with finality as he turned and walked out the door. Devon listened to them as he moved down the corridor, her heart cracking gradually as each step became more and more distant. Only when she couldn't hear them any more did she yield to the sobs that tortured her soul.

11

━━∾⊶❀∽❀∽❀∽❀∽❀∽❀∾━━

It's for Sunday, the third of April," Gayle whispered, covering the mouthpiece of the telephone as she perched on the edge of the counter in Devon's kitchen. "Listen, you know I'm game for just about anything, but three parties in three nights? I don't think we can do it."

Devon looked up from her checkbook. "We have to. I still owe more than seven thousand dollars in past debts. I'd give you the exact figure, but I think it would give you a nervous breakdown." She nodded at the telephone. "Accept it."

Gayle gave her an exasperated look. "You're going to kill me. I'm going to die of exhaustion before my thirtieth birthday."

"Close your eyes and picture dollar bills floating down from heaven. You'll make it."

She turned back to her checkbook. In all honesty, visions of dollar bills had been the only thing that got her through the last four weeks. Callahan's fundraiser *had* been a turning point. It had brought her a sense of loss that was beyond tears—she hadn't cried since Clay

157

walked out of the kitchen—but it had also been the major boost the business needed. The meal, at least, had been a flawless accomplishment that night. People had sat up and taken notice, especially when they learned that Callahan's election committee hadn't been charged an exorbitant price for the sole, asparagus, and *spanakopita* pastries. In the weeks since, acquaintances and strangers alike had hired her to cater their affairs. Those who were her acquaintances were the hardest to handle; time and time again she had been forced to put her pride on the line, but oddly, it didn't matter anymore. Nothing mattered but digging out from under her pile of debts.

Nothing mattered because Clay was gone.

She stared down at her checkbook unseeingly, the misery of that night still haunting her. She had to stop doing this to herself. Every thought she had seemed to circle back to Clay somehow. And then the raw pain that had been wrapped around her heart would start squirming again until it was unbearable. Her only salvation was in not thinking. Because when she thought, the same useless realizations kept coming back to torment her.

Moira had been right. She had known what she was getting into, and she had no one to blame but herself. Clay Wyatt could not see past his conditioning, his hang-ups. He wasn't capable of loving wholly. Now that he knew she was broke, he was undoubtedly convinced that she had been after him for his money.

Devon groaned and pressed her fingers to her temples to try to still her pounding headache. Stop it, she ordered herself. Don't think. Work.

A movement at her side alerted her to the fact that Gayle had left the counter and was standing beside her. She glanced up at Gayle with a look of blank exhaustion.

"Well?" Devon asked. "Did you accept the job on the third?"

Gayle shook her head.

"No? Why not?" Her voice spiraled upward with the beginnings of hysteria. She heard it and forced herself to relax.

Gayle, however, was not above commenting on it. "That's why not," she answered, pulling out another chair and sitting down across from her. "I told the guy I'd call him back. I think we should talk first."

Talk. Unfortunately, she thought, her life was too empty to discuss. "There's nothing to talk about," she responded. "I need the money. Case closed."

"No one's going to be able to chase you into your grave for the money you owe them."

Devon raised an eyebrow at her, then quickly schooled her features into neutrality again. It was a gesture she had picked up from Clay. She felt a brief flash of bitter pain. "Is this going to be a lecture?" she managed.

"Of the first degree. You might as well sit back and listen to me, because I'm not going to shut up."

Devon did as she was told, trying to force a wry smile to her lips. "In that case, go ahead. Let's get it over with so we can call this guy back and accept the job."

Gayle groaned. "Look, I don't know what happened the night of that fundraiser, but it's done a number on you. You've been quiet, withdrawn."

"People have moods. Women have moods. Maybe it's my hormones or something."

"For four weeks?" Gayle scoffed.

"Will you accept a life-threatening disease?"

"Oh, Devon, stop it. I'm serious."

Devon sighed and leaned against the table again, resting her chin in her hands. "I am too. I'm serious about not wanting to talk about it."

"That's not hard to figure out. But will you at least promise me that you'll think about it? Being quiet and withdrawn is one thing, but you're running yourself right into the ground. Your interest in the business has been more like an obsession lately. You've had these debts for sixteen months, Devon. Why do you have to wipe them out in a single week now? I mean, look at you. You look like hell, if you don't mind my saying so."

"I do," Devon responded shortly. "I mind very much." She didn't need reminding.

"You've got caverns under your eyes," Gayle rushed on, refusing to be stifled. "You shake a lot. You're chain-smoking, and I never even saw you light a cigarette before. You're falling apart at the seams. I know you can't afford a vacation, but for God's sake, give yourself a break and relax for a week."

"That," Devon replied honestly enough, "is absolutely the worst thing I could do to myself right now. You think I've been bad lately? You'd be visiting me in a mental institution after a week off." She jumped to her feet with restless energy. "Where's that guy's number?" she demanded, rummaging through the papers on the counter.

"What happened that night?" Gayle asked abruptly.

"Nothing surprising," Devon answered shortly. "Come on, Gayle, what did you do with that number? It's not here."

Gayle gave her a stubborn grin. "I know it's not. It's in my pocket. I'm going out to pick up some hamburgers. My treat. After I see you eat one, I'll consider giving you the number." She got up and headed for the door. "Cheese? Catsup? Mustard?"

Devon glowered at her. "None of the above. Including the hamburger. Don't waste your money. I'm not hungry."

Gayle rolled her eyes. "Hungry or not, you're going to eat or I'm not going to give you the phone number. I'll bring you back one with everything on it. You need the calories."

"Damn it, Gayle! I'll fire you!"

"No, you won't. You won't find anyone else to work as cheaply as I do." She gave Devon one last grin and slammed the door behind her.

Devon sighed and dropped down on the chair again, pressing her fingers to her temples. What had she been doing? Writing checks. Whittling away at bills. She reached for her pen again, then jumped as the telephone rang.

She leaned back in her chair and grabbed for it. At

least it was no longer absurd to hope that it might be a job. "Hello?"

"Devon Jordan?" The man's voice was deep and polished. It had a familiar ring, but she couldn't quite place it.

"Yes?"

"My name is Mr. Blalock." She frowned. She didn't know a Mr. Blalock. "I called a little while ago and spoke to one of your employees about catering an affair on the third of April," he went on. "I was told that you would get back to me, but quite frankly, my employer is anxious to know if you'll do the job."

A slow grin touched Devon's lips. She looked at the door Gayle had disappeared through and stuck her tongue out at it. "Of course I will. Just give me the details. What kind of an affair is it?"

"It's an afternoon function. Sandwiches and that sort of thing will suffice, I'm sure."

"How many people?"

"I've estimated thirty. Beverages are important. It's a tennis gathering."

Devon nodded. "Outside, then?"

"Yes."

"And light snacks. Nothing filling."

"Precisely."

"I'll work up a menu, Mr. Blalock, and get back to you with it. I'll be able to give you an idea of the cost then. From what you've told me, it sounds as though a buffet table would be suitable. This shouldn't run you a lot of money."

"My employer has instructed me to spare no expense."

Devon was momentarily nonplussed. "Well . . . okay. Why don't you give me your number, and I'll get back to you as soon as possible?"

"Fine. It's 555-1219."

Devon started scribbling down the number. She got as far as the "two" before the pencil dropped from her hand. She was trembling again. "Could you . . . uh, could you repeat that?"

"555-1219."

Clay's number. What was he up to? She hadn't heard from him in a month. What was he doing? Fear and anger gripped her.

"Sorry," she ground out. "The deal's off."

There was a short, confused silence. "Excuse me?" he asked, and now she was able to place the voice perfectly. The man's first name was Joseph. Clay's butler. He had greeted her at Clay's door a hundred times. No wonder she hadn't recognized his voice immediately. It used to sound warm.

Oh, God, she was going to be sick. Why was he doing this to her? The room started spinning, and she was suddenly afraid she was going to faint. She had to get off the phone.

"The deal is off," she repeated as succinctly as she could manage. "You can tell your extravagant employer that I'm not interested." She slammed the phone down again before he could respond.

She crossed her arms on the table and laid her head down on them, trying to take deep, even breaths. Clay. Why? She groaned helplessly and sat up to reach for another cigarette.

Gayle burst in just as she lit it. She took in Devon's ashen face as she dropped the bag of hamburgers on the table. "Hey, look, don't fall apart over this." She dug in her pocket. "Here. Call him, if it means that much to you."

Devon reached out slowly and took the piece of paper from her hand. Then she methodically tore it into little pieces. Gayle gaped at her.

"What the hell are you doing?"

"He called back while you were gone," Devon answered hollowly. "We're not going to take the job."

Gayle made an admirable attempt to hide the horror in her eyes. "Devon, for God's sake, it's okay. There'll be other jobs. Are you all right? You don't look good."

"I'm not good. I—" She broke off. For the first time since the night of the fundraiser, tears were choking her. She could feel the flimsy control she had been clinging to for four weeks slowly sliding through her fingers. "I—" she tried again, then jumped up from the table, smothering a sob.

"Oh, no," Gayle breathed, reaching out to grab her arm as she started to flee toward the bedroom. "What is it? Did something else happen while I was gone? What—" Suddenly the telephone began shrilling again. Gayle turned to give it a frantic look, and Devon pulled away from her.

"Answer it," she whispered in a tremulous voice. "I'll be fine. Just give me a minute or two alone." When Gayle made no move toward the telephone, she forced more strength into her tone. "Go on, answer it. I'll be in my bedroom." She started to turn away, then paused. "Just one thing. If it has anything to do with a tennis party given by Clayton Wyatt, don't take it. I don't care what the guy says to you, don't take it." She turned on her heel and slammed the bedroom door behind her.

She sat down shakily on the bed. How could he? Why would he? Her head spun. She groaned again and flopped down on her back, her shock and pain yielding to fury.

Gayle's soft knock at her door interrupted her just as she was pounding her fist into her pillow. She jumped up again and flung open the door.

"It's him," Gayle breathed.

"Him?" She knew who, of course, but she couldn't believe he would push it.

"That Clayton Wyatt you told me not to accept the party from. He won't take no for an answer. He's demanding to speak to you. I'm sorry."

Her mouth twisted into an ugly smile. "Don't be sorry. I'll take it." She pushed past Gayle and stormed into the kitchen. "That bastard," she muttered.

"Do you want me to leave?" Gayle asked uncertainly from the bedroom door.

"That," Devon answered darkly, "depends entirely upon how well you weather storms."

"Uh, I think I'll see you tomorrow."

Devon waited until Gayle had closed the door behind her; then she whirled back to the phone and grabbed the receiver. "What the hell do you think you're up to?" she demanded.

She was unprepared for the sound of his voice again. It had been so long, a whole month. Dark and velvety, it touched the deepest part of her soul as though she had just heard it yesterday. Devon squeezed her eyes shut and steeled herself against it.

"Nothing fancy," he responded dryly. "As Joseph told you, I'm giving a party on the third. You've developed quite a reputation for being one of the best caterers in the valley. Since I always deal with the best, I'd like you to cater it."

"That shouldn't surprise me," she hissed. "I've never known you to get your hands dirty by dealing with anyone who was less than perfect."

"Not intentionally, at any rate," he drawled sarcastically.

Devon caught her breath. His voice was so cold, so hard, that she wondered how she had ever thought him sensitive. "You don't want me to cater your damned party," she snapped. "You're just too neurotic and infantile to let sleeping dogs lie. It's over, Clay. You've made it perfectly clear how you feel about me, so grow up and leave it alone. Revenge doesn't become you."

"Don't flatter yourself. Revenge is the least of my concerns. I just want to throw a good party on the third."

A good party. She'd been killing herself, trying to bury herself in the business, and he was worried about parties. Her heart seethed with anger and humiliation.

"Fine," she answered, her voice icy. "You go throw yourself one hell of a party. Just do it without me."

There was a short silence. His voice came back as cool and neutral as if he had been conducting a board meeting. "I'm serious about this, Devon. I want you to cater the party."

"If you were serious about it, you would have called me yourself instead of trying to trick me. What was the scenario supposed to be, Clay? Did you think you could keep your identity in the dark until I showed up on your doorstep replete with goodies?"

"Chores such as hiring caterers fall under Joseph's jurisdiction," he answered coldly. "I had no ulterior motive when I asked him to call you."

"Like hell you didn't. If you had no ulterior motives, you would have called one of the other five hundred caterers in the valley capable of throwing together sandwiches." She took a deep breath, then finished in a voice taut with rage. "Listen to me, Clay, and listen to me good. I may be broke. I may not be up to your standards. But I . . . am not . . . stupid! There's a real reason you want me to cater this party, and it's probably the same reason you had your butler call to arrange it. I want to know what it is."

A tense silence filled the line. "Fair enough," he responded eventually. "I didn't call you myself because you would have refused the job unequivocally, no questions asked."

"I'm refusing it unequivocally anyway, so you might as well keep talking and tell me your motives. What is it, Clay? Are you operating under some perverse desire to put me in my place? Will you get some kind of warped kick out of seeing me run around your house with the hired help. *What?*" she demanded.

"You're way off base," he answered tightly.

"Am I? I don't think so. I think your poor, fragile ego has been bruised because you almost fell for someone who quite possibly could have wanted you for your money. I think you want revenge. You know, Clay, if it means that much to you, I could always do this up for you right. I might be able to dig up a French maid's costume for the affair. Would that soothe your ego?"

Clay chuckled humorlessly. "Why not? If you want to dress up like a French maid, I'm certainly not going to stop you."

"Damn you," she breathed.

"Well, you surprise me. I've never known you to have an ego in that respect. In the entire time I've known you, you've never held any great reverence for social position. I suppose it never occurred to me that you might be embarrassed to do the job. You worked the fundraiser when you knew that all your old friends would be there."

Devon stiffened, her heart thudding sickly. I didn't love the man who hired me for the fundraiser, she thought wildly. Instead, she answered coldly, "I never slept with the other people I worked for." She shivered, thinking how close she had come on so many occasions to telling him she loved him. I'd gag over the words now, she thought vehemently.

"Well," he countered cruelly, "you *did* sleep with me, so I'm willing to make it worth your while."

"What are you saying?" she whispered.

"I'm offering you fifteen hundred dollars to cater the tennis party. Is that enough to take care of your ego?"

Devon paled. She collapsed on a nearby chair. "You bastard," she breathed.

His voice became even more contemptuous. She hadn't thought it was possible. "Go ahead, Devon. Accept it. We've got no secrets anymore, remember? It's okay. Women's mercenary tendencies neither surprise nor upset me anymore."

A deadly calm overtook her. She stood up again slowly. "That's good," she replied calmly, "because you just bought yourself a fifteen-hundred-dollar lunch."

She hung up before he had a chance to respond. Her rage was a cold, hard shield around her heart. She reached for a cookbook and sat down hard at the table again. Lunch, hell. For fifteen hundred dollars, he was

166

going to get a six-course dinner. The only person who was going to make a profit on this was her supplier. She flipped through the cookbook, her smile dangerously placid.

All in all, she thought, hating him was a lot easier than loving him.

12

~~∞∞∞∞∞∞∞∞∞∞~~

Is this what you wanted?" Gayle held out the French maid's uniform doubtfully.

Devon turned away from her bedroom mirror, where she had been putting the finishing touches on her chignon. "You found one!"

Gayle walked into the room and dropped the uniform on the bed. "I guess that means this *is* what you wanted." She gave Devon a searching look. "What are you up to?"

Devon turned her attention back to the mirror. "Does it matter? I'm not quiet and withdrawn anymore, am I?"

"No, but you've been reminding me of a manic depressive. I'm not sure which scares me the most." She dropped down on the bed. "You're sure you want to do this party alone? I've got all afternoon free. Doug took the kids to visit his mother. I'm virtually a single woman for the next four hours or so."

"No, I want to do this alone. I *have* to handle this on my own." She left the mirror and started to dress. "Personal pride, and all that," she explained, trying to dredge up a smile. "Besides, it's just a buffet. It's a one-person job."

"Just a buffet!" Gayle hooted. "Caviar, lobster-stuffed mushrooms, a champagne fountain, and beef bourguignon?"

Devon forced herself to shrug as she pulled on sheer black panty hose. "I'm just giving the man what he paid for," she reminded her. "You don't happen to have a garter belt, do you? No, never mind. There's no time for you to run home for it, anyway. But it would be a nice touch. It would really round out the ensemble, don't you think?"

Gayle stared at her. "I don't own a garter belt, you don't own regular stockings, and there's no way I'm going to run around out in that heat looking for any either. I did my duty with the costume." She paused, then asked abruptly, "Why are you giving this guy what he paid for instead of pocketing the profit? Dollar bills drifting down from heaven and all that, remember? Shall I quote you?"

"Don't bother. I told you, it's a matter of personal pride. Is everything in the car?"

Gayle nodded.

"And you'll follow me and help me get it all inside?"

Gayle nodded again.

Devon took a deep, steadying breath and checked herself in the mirror one last time. Her eyes were unnaturally bright. "Okay," she breathed. "Let's do it."

It was worse than she had feared. Clay's tennis court, pool, and patio was virtually filled with people who had known her for years. It was like a macabre version of *This Is Your Life*. Had he done this to her on purpose? Devon shuddered as she remembered the cold hardness of his voice when she had last spoken to him on the telephone. It was possible. Anything was possible with this vindictive stranger she had once fancied herself in love with.

She closed her eyes and counted slowly to ten in a vain effort to control her burgeoning anger. She'd ruin everything if she launched herself at him in fury the minute she laid eyes on him. The success of her revenge hinged upon her being cool. It was, however, a difficult facade to maintain. The anticipation of finally meeting him face to face again was torturing her and prodding her temper.

Clay hadn't left the tennis court since she'd arrived. Joseph had met her at the door, his expression meticulously blank, and had instructed her where to set up the buffet table. She'd indeed been relegated to the world of the hired help. It galled her more than she'd ever dreamed possible.

She leaned against one of the columns of the patio and watched Clay through narrowed eyes. Now he was playing a game of mixed doubles. His partner was the only person at the party she didn't know, and Clay had been showing the woman more than a small amount of attention, constantly touching her arm or dropping his own arm over her shoulders. Is he deliberately trying to antagonize me, Devon wondered, or has he replaced me already? She choked back the anger crowding her throat and turned to check on the buffet table, unable to watch him anymore.

The buffet had successfully elicited the surprise and the jokes she had intended. Moira's reaction was typical. She arrived through the sliding glass doors from the family room and promptly abandoned Derrick when she spotted Devon.

Moira took in the French maid's costume and gapped at Devon. "What are you doing?" she breathed, then she glanced down at the buffet table. "What the hell? Is this your doing, or has Clay suddenly become ostentatious?"

"Actually, he's become vicious and vengeful," Devon answered hollowly. "But I'll settle for people thinking he's ostentatious."

Moira grimaced. "In other words, it's war. God, Devon, I feel so bad about this. I can't believe he would sink this low." She glanced around at the crowd, taking in all the familiar faces. "After seeing you two together those few times, I actually let myself start hoping I was wrong about him," she murmured.

"Well, you weren't," Devon answered flatly. "But at least you tried to warn me."

Another woman stepped up to the buffet table behind Moira. "Oh, good grief what's this?" she asked in surprise. She cast a suspicious look toward Clay out on the tennis court. "I thought he said this was supposed to be casual."

Moira turned to her. "I haven't tried anything yet, but I'd hazard a guess that this is probably the best beef bourguignon you've had in your life," she answered. "And as for Clay, maybe this is as subtle and casual as he knows how to be."

The woman glanced up at her, then her eyes fell on Devon. "Oh, you're responsible for all this."

Devon crossed her arms over her chest and leaned back against the column again. "No, I just cooked it. Clay is responsible for everything else."

The woman looked doubtful. "He is?" Then, for the first time, she seemed to notice what Devon was wearing. "You're hiring out as a maid now too? I'd heard you were catering, of course, but I didn't realize things were *that* bad." She paused, then gave her a conspiratorial smile. "Just how bad are they?"

Moira opened her mouth, but Devon placed a restraining hand on her arm. "Down, comrade," she whispered, then answered the other woman. "Not bad at all. Actually, I've been doing just fine with the catering lately, now that a few of you folks have remembered my name again. I'm not hiring out as a maid. The costume is something Clay asked for." Did he ever, she thought. God, she was getting to be a wizard at telling half-truths.

The woman nodded uncertainly, filled her plate, and moved away. Moira whirled back to Devon. "It amazes me how few manners some of these people have!" she exclaimed heatedly. "What a bunch of frustrated, insensitive gossipmongers!"

Devon shrugged, but her nonchalance was forced. Her temper seethed. "Well, I think I ought to develop a thick skin real fast," she answered. "Something tells me that that won't be the last time this happens today."

Moira threw an angry look out at the crowd. "It looks as though they've been handpicked for optimum embarrassment value."

"I don't doubt it."

Moira gave her a long look as she digested Devon's words, then demanded suddenly, "*Did* Clay ask you to wear that get-up?"

"Actually, he more or less dared me to. The guests, however, are all his doing."

Before Moira could respond, another woman stepped up to the buffet table. "Devon? I thought that was you. I'd heard you were doing this sort of thing after Ian left you."

Devon gave the woman a level look. "You don't have the inside track on the story, Elizabeth," she answered.

"I don't?"

"No. Ian didn't leave me. I left him. Now run along back to the party and fill everyone in." She couldn't keep the bite out of her voice.

Elizabeth gave her a cold look. "You'll have to do that yourself. Todd and I have the court now. I just came over to see what you'd dished up here. Would you mind filling a plate for me, honey, and leaving it by the pool where the Arnolds are sitting?"

"The mushrooms are best when they're warm."

The woman looked down at the buffet table for the first time. "Oh," she answered, her face blank with confusion. "Why in the world would Clay serve something like this for a tennis party?"

Devon shrugged. "I don't know. I guess he just likes to show off."

Elizabeth shook her head unbelievingly and turned away. Moira reached angrily for a plate. "I'll do it," she snapped.

Devon pulled the plate from her hand. "No, you won't. I have to do this myself."

"I'd like to pour the entire fountain of champagne over Clay's head," Moira muttered.

Devon began filling the plate for Elizabeth. "Would you settle for telling me who the brunette is?" she asked, keeping one eye on the court. Clay and his partner were walking off. His arm was around her waist. Moira looked over at them and scowled.

"That's Senator Callahan's daughter."

Recognition filtered slowly through the tight web of Devon's control. "I thought she looked familiar," she murmured finally. "I've seen her picture in the papers. She's even more beautiful in person."

Moira gave her a sharp look. "I don't think Clay's dating her, if that's what you're thinking. Nobody's seen hide nor hair of him since the fundraiser, and they're both such notable figures that if they *had* been seen together, word would have gotten around. But no one's seen Clay. We didn't even know if he was still among the living until we got the summons to appear here today."

Devon flinched slightly. Despite Moira's assurances, jealousy clawed at her heart like a wild animal as she watched them. "Well," she said, "it wouldn't surprise me if he *was* dating her. God knows she's wealthy enough for him, what with all the Callahan money behind her. And we both know how Clay Wyatt feels about women and money. Nothing else is even remotely important as long as they've got their own and he can be sure they're not interested in his."

"Oh, Devon, don't . . ." Moira began, but she trailed off as Devon shook her head vehemently and started across the lawn with Elizabeth's plate.

Her heart pounded and her headache throbbed as she made her way toward the Arnolds' table. Damn this headache, she thought. It seemed as though it had been with her for months. Some days it would fade away, but it always came back stronger than ever. And now, when she most needed to be bright and alert, it was so bad that it seemed to cloud her vision.

Unfortunately, it didn't cloud it so much that she couldn't see Clay and Senator Callahan's daughter standing right in her path.

She paused briefly to steady herself, then forced herself to walk up to them. "Mr. Wyatt," she purred. "I trust you've found everything up to your usual standards?"

He seemed to stiffen at the sound of her voice. A single heartbeat pounded in her ears before he turned to look at her. A brief flash of amusement showed in his eyes as he took in her costume; then a cold, hard mask seemed to descend over his features. "So far," he drawled, "everything appears to be just the way I wanted it."

She cringed a bit at the scorn in his tone. The battle lines were drawn, she realized grimly. He was no longer even pretending that he hadn't intended to embarrass her. She nodded and started to step around him.

"Where are you going with that?" he demanded.

Devon froze and looked back at him. "With what?"

He nodded toward the plate she held.

"Oh, this. Don't worry. I'm not going to sit down and eat on the job. It's for Elizabeth Tanley. Obviously she's not content with a buffet. She wants service."

He frowned but said nothing.

"Isn't that what you wanted me to do? Serve your guests in a manner that lives up to that formidable reputation of mine that you told me about?" she asked innocently.

He suddenly reached for the plate. "Give me that," he growled.

Devon stepped adroitly out of reach. "Oh, no, Mr. Wyatt. I couldn't let you take it to her. That's *my* job." Sarcasm made her voice razor-sharp.

Anger began to harden his features even more. Then he glanced down at the plate again. His expression changed to one of astonishment. "What the hell is that?" he demanded.

Devon looked down at the caviar, mushrooms, and beef, then glanced up again to smile at him sweetly. "Oh, about fifteen hundred dollars," she answered, turning away.

She didn't dare look back at him as she made her way to the Arnolds' table, and when she turned around again, he was gone. A quick survey of the patio found him talking animatedly with the first woman who had interrupted her and Moira. Devon changed direction so that she could walk close enough to them to overhear their conversation.

Clay's voice was so low with anger that she almost missed it. "I am *not* trying to impress anyone, Lucille. The meal was . . . is . . . the damned thing's a mistake."

Devon smiled secretively and turned back to the buffet table. Oh, yes, she thought, the war was on.

A crowd was beginning to gather around the table. She positioned herself nearby, still smiling.

"I never thought I'd hear myself say this, but I think I would have preferred beer to champagne. What's gotten into Wyatt today?"

"I don't know, but I know what's gone *out* of him—his tennis game. I've never seen him play so poorly."

"Something must be bothering him. He seems so preoccupied lately."

"How would you know? No one's seen him for a month."

"Maybe he's been holed up with Callahan's daughter. Maybe she's just knocked him off his feet."

Devon's smile turned brittle, then died. Another flash of jealousy scorched her; she bit her lip and moved away from the table. She'd learned all she needed to know. People were talking. She'd gotten her revenge.

Suddenly she felt empty and drained. It was all over. He'd tried to get even with her, and she'd fought back. End of chapter. She knew, deep in her heart, that they'd never tangle again. It wouldn't be an ongoing war. Just one massive battle, winner take all.

She headed listlessly for the kitchen to start cleaning

things up. She wanted to make a quick exit when the party was over. She hoped that it would be soon. Odd, she thought. She'd expected to feel exhilarated when it was all done with. He'd tried to hurt her, and she had made him look foolish for his efforts. She should feel proud, satisfied. Instead, she felt miserable.

Trying to ignore the agonizing sob that was caught in her throat, she started to wash up. At that point she wanted nothing more out of life than a dark room and a bed. Maybe Gayle was right. Maybe she should take a week off, she thought. She'd been living under a thundercloud of tension for so long; now that it had finally floated away, she felt deflated, lifeless.

She finished cleaning up, dried her hands, and looked down at her watch. It was twenty past six. People *had* to be finished eating by now, and once the food was gone, she'd have every right to leave. Crossing her fingers, she went back outside.

The crowd had thinned by roughly half. The diehards, including Clay and the senator's daughter, were clustered by the pool. They had taken ice buckets full of wine and several coolers of beer with them. The champagne fountain was dry and the food, what little there was left of it, had been abandoned. Devon heaved a sigh of relief and went to start clearing off the buffet table.

"There she is!" The raucous male voice caught her attention immediately. Somehow she knew it was aimed at her. She felt sick as she realized that the group at the pool had been talking about her.

She took a long, exhausted breath, then forced herself to look up. Roger Staniel. She had never liked him. He was an obnoxious, boisterous man who made a habit of drinking too much. Ironically, he couldn't hold his alcohol at all, and tonight was no exception. He lurched up from his chair and began staggering toward her. Devon felt her heart constrict. She knew before he reached her that he meant trouble. The little hairs on the back of her neck seemed to pick up as she stepped stoically out of the shadows and into the last of the sunlight.

The crowd hushed as he approached her. The quiet made his voice seem unnaturally loud. "How's it going, sweetheart?" he called out to her. His attempt at a cavalier swagger was ruined by the fact that he was having trouble walking straight.

"Just fine, Roger," she answered softly. Don't antagonize him, she warned herself. Maybe he'll get bored and stagger away again if he can't get a rise out of you.

But he didn't stagger away. He popped a cold mushroom into his mouth and leaned heavily against the table as he washed it down with a mouthful of beer.

"You been doing this kind of thing a lot lately, huh?" he asked. "Can't be much money in it."

"I do all right," she murmured, clasping her hands tightly in front of her. They itched to reach out and slap him for the spectacle he was trying to make of her.

"Yeah? Dressing up like that helps, huh?"

She colored fiercely as she glanced down at the short maid's costume. Now was not the time to worry about embarrassing Clay, she thought. She forced herself to shrug. "It was a joke," she told him quietly.

Roger chuckled lasciviously. "You make a little money on the side that way?"

Devon stiffened. "Pardon me?" No, he couldn't have said that, she thought wildly. He couldn't mean what she thought he meant.

"I asked you," he bellowed, leaning a little closer to her until the smell of alcohol on his breath almost sickened her, "if you make extra money dressing up like that." Then he laughed uproariously. "Or taking it off, as the case may be. Must be tough, huh? Falling out of the old gilded cage, I mean. You were so high and mighty, weren't you, looking down your nose at all of us? Now look what happened to you. Your husband dumps you and you're down on your back trying to make a few extra bucks. You ain't so high and mighty any more, are you?"

A shudder of humiliation passed through her. She opened her mouth to speak, but no words would come. Suddenly he grabbed her arm. "Come on, sweetheart," he went on, grinning at her as he tried to pull her toward the house. "I'm good for a few bucks. You sure wouldn't give me the time of day while you were sitting on top of the world."

Slowly, dangerously, her mortification transformed itself into rage. She pulled away from his drunken grasp with deadly calm. "There's not enough money in the world to get me within ten feet of you," she whispered. "Now go sit down and we'll forget all about this. With any luck, I'll never lay eyes on you again as long as I live."

He lurched backward, losing his balance slightly as she jerked away from him. His expression twisted into an ugly smile, and he opened his mouth to answer. Then his jaw dropped open. His gaze flew to a spot over Devon's shoulder and he froze.

Devon sensed Clay drawing his fist back before she saw him. Her fury exploded within her like a million firecrackers gone haywire. She spun around to face him, stepping in front of Roger.

"Don't even think about it," she breathed venomously. "It's a little too late to switch loyalties now, isn't it? You got what you wanted, you bastard. You saw me embarrassed. Now go back to the pool and take your bows. I'll handle this. I don't need your help."

A muscle twitched crazily in his jaw, but he slowly dropped his fist. "Devon . . ." he began.

"Go . . . to . . . hell," she interrupted him, then she whirled back to Roger. "I'd appreciate it if you'd join him."

She felt her palm make contact with the man's cheek even before she knew that she was going to strike him. Shattered, she stifled a sob and turned on her heel to flee inside.

Clay caught up to her in the living room. Out of habit, and because she had known it would be safe there, she had left her purse behind the bar. She heard his footsteps on the tile floor, slow and unsure, and she stiffened. Her purse in her hand, she straightened and turned to face him.

"Don't," she warned him, her voice trembling over unshed tears. "Don't say a word. Go back to your party. Leave me alone."

His broad shoulders heaved as he breathed. "I'm sorry," he said finally.

"Now's a fine time to start feeling that way."

"You lied to me!" he bellowed.

"I didn't want to lose you!"

"You hurt me!"

"I loved you!"

She screamed the words. They echoed against the massive boundaries of the room. Then, as he stared at her through the shadows and dim golden glow of the single overhead light, she crumbled. She stumbled back against the wall and, as her back made contact with it, she slowly slid downward until she sat down hard on the tiled floor. The sobs she had been holding back for four weeks claimed her. She rested her head against her updrawn knees and wept.

She was unaware of Clay moving behind the bar. She was drowning in an unfathomable pain that she had been battling for what seemed like forever. Now it had caught her and it wouldn't let her go. Her sobs shook her, and she rocked gently back and forth under the weight of them.

"Loved me? Past tense?"

She raised her head to find him sitting on the floor beside her. "Look at me," she managed to say. "Do I look as if I'm in any condition to discern the difference at the moment?"

"It matters. Try."

She shook her head. "Why?" she demanded. Her voice was vicious with pain. "You got your revenge. Go on outside and shake hands with Roger Staniel and gloat. You've got it coming to you." She took a deep, convulsive breath and laughed thinly. "I thought I won. I thought I turned the tables on you. But I didn't. You got me in the end."

"Devon, stop it." His expression was that of a man

179

who had just been punched in the stomach. "I didn't mean it to turn out this way."

"You were after revenge."

He took a deep, unsteady breath. "Yes," he admitted hoarsely. "I was after revenge. I wanted to get even with you for lying to me. I spent weeks trying to cope with what you had done, with losing you. I thought that if I could just get back at you, I could forget it all."

She held a trembling hand out to him. "Well then, shake. Congratulations. You did it."

He pushed her hand away and laughed raggedly. "No—no, I didn't. You were right. I tried to demean you. What I never could admit to myself was that you couldn't be demeaned. What I tried to do to you was impossible. You're a lady with one hell of a lot of class, more than all those socialites out there put together. I tried to embarrass you, and you ended up making me look like a fool. A stupid fool."

She gazed at him through murky eyes that couldn't cope with much more. "Oh, God, Clay," she moaned. "Why? Do you hate me that much?"

He chuckled, and the sound was hollow. "Hate you? No, loving you was the problem. I wanted you to hurt as badly as I did when I found out I was loving a lie."

"You weren't loving a lie! Everything you saw, every emotion I gave you, was real! The only things I omitted were the things that made me the way I am!"

Clay reached up unsteadily for a bottle of bourbon that sat on the bar. "Can you stand this stuff straight?" he asked, seeming to change the subject.

Devon nodded miserably and took the bottle from him. She swallowed from it, then handed it back to him. "Thanks. I guess I needed that."

"Have some more."

"Are you trying to get me drunk or something? It'll take more than that bottle." She shivered. "Even my bones feel cold. Damn you, and damn Roger."

Clay flinched as though she had slapped him. "I'm not

trying to get you drunk. I'm trying to get you to relax and talk."

"Talk?"

"About those things you omitted. The things that make you the way you are."

She gave him a wary look and took another swallow of bourbon. "I don't want to talk about them."

"You owe me. You told me lies. Now I want to hear the truth."

She let out a shaky sigh. The silence between them became almost unbearable before she said, "Okay." She put the bottle to her lips again, then propped it up between her knees.

"You're not the only one who got robbed," she whispered, staring out at the city lights. "You don't have a monopoly on being used. You've been so busy making every woman you meet pay for your ex-wife's sins that you never stopped to think about it."

"Think about what?"

"That when a marriage dissolves, it doesn't have to be the husband who gets taken to the cleaner's!" she snapped, then swallowed hard. "Ian—my ex-husband— was a close friend of my father's. The executor of my parents' wills, actually. I told you they were killed in a car accident when I was nineteen." Clay nodded silently, and she pushed on. "I more or less had a very privileged and sheltered childhood. I was devastated when my parents were killed. Didn't know what to do, how to handle anything, from the funeral on down. Ian took care of everything. I ended up depending on him totally, just as I had once depended on my mom and dad. "Naiveté, I think they call it."

She cast him a sardonic smile, but he didn't respond.

"Well, anyway, Ian had no trouble convincing me to marry him and move out here with him. What I didn't know at the time was that he had long been in love with someone else. And . . ." She paused, taking a deep breath. "And that he had a severe gambling problem. I

181

mean *severe*. It was so bad that he had actually married me for my inheritance. He thought he could clean up his gambling debts, divorce me, then marry Janice."

"You knew her?"

"I knew her name. He spared no details when push finally came to shove and the cards were laid on the table."

"Go on."

"There's not much more to tell. Needless to say he never stopped gambling, and instead of cleaning up his debts, he just made them worse. We were married for six years. That gave him a lot of time to make those debts astronomical. When I found out the truth, I left him. But by that time, everything we owned had to be sold. He'd run through roughly a million dollars of my parents' money, and then some. I had to sell everything to cover the debts. There was no money left for me to go back to college. So I fell back on the one thing I knew how to do well, the one thing I had learned while cavorting around with your friends out there by the pool. I was always one hell of a hostess. So I put that know-how into a catering business. You know the rest."

"Why didn't you tell me?"

She looked at him disbelievingly. "Because of Gina. Because of your ex-wife. I didn't think you could handle my poverty, and I was right. Besides, let's be fair about this. I *did* try to tell you—that day at the zoo. You weren't having any of it." She picked up the bottle of bourbon again and took another mouthful.

When the silence between them stretched out, she cast him a wary look. "You're not going to argue the point?"

"How can I? You did try to tell me, and I wouldn't listen. I'd sound like a fool if I tried to argue that. And as for not being able to handle your poverty, would you believe me if I told you that that wasn't true?"

She thought about it a moment. "No. No, I know your problems as though they were my own at this point."

Clay smiled sardonically. "You probably know them better than I do. You saw them before I did, and tried to

protect us against them. You were right. My distrust of
women and my hang-ups regarding my money have
virtually ruled my life for the last several years. I vowed
that I was never going to allow what Gina did to me to
happen again, and I guess I got obsessed by that.
Devon," he said suddenly, turning to her. His hands
found her shoulders, and she shivered as warmth finally
touched her bones.

"Don't," she whispered. "Don't touch me. I can't think
straight when you touch me."

"You don't have to think straight. You just have to
listen. I love you. I love you more than I do my money.
I'd give up everything tomorrow if you'd just come back
to me and give me another chance. The last four weeks
have been hell without you. I didn't know how much I
cherished having you here until you were gone."

Slowly, gradually, the warmth inside her spread. It
pushed at the ice in the pit of her stomach. Peace started
to settle over her, wiping away her fatigue. She managed
to grin at him.

"Well," she answered, "now that you mention it, I do
have a favorite charity that would be overjoyed to get
your money. That is, if you're serious about what you just
told me."

Clay blanched. Devon struggled to keep a straight face
as she held the bottle of bourbon out to him. "Do you
need this?" she asked innocently.

He didn't answer but simply grabbed the bottle from
her hand and took a hefty swallow. She couldn't stand it
anymore. An ecstatic happiness bubbled over in the
laugh that escaped her.

"Oh, Clay," she whispered as her laughter dissolved.
She reached for him and wrapped her arms around his
neck. Burying her face against his shoulder, she murmured, "It's not the money. It's not whether or not you
have it that's the point. The important thing is that you
don't let it affect us."

His arms closed around her. "You don't want me to
give anything away?"

"Of course not. I have nothing against Rolls-Royces and cabins in Colorado. Trust me when I tell you that poverty does *not* breed character."

His response was a thorough kiss. "Stay with me tonight," he said suddenly. "Let me get rid of these people, and stay. We'll talk until the sun comes up."

"Talk?"

"Among other things. But we need to talk. We haven't done nearly enough of that. Just say you'll stay, Devon. Stay tonight and tomorrow night and . . ." He trailed off to kiss her again.

"Do I dare hope that your offer to have me move in has been reinstated?" She grinned at him happily. "I should warn you that you ought to be prepared for me to say yes this time. The only reason I couldn't give you an answer before was because I couldn't bear to start a life with you without telling you the truth first."

Clay's smile faded at the memory of what she had done to him. Devon held her breath. Then his mouth descended on hers once again and he held her more tightly. "I'm more than prepared to have you say yes," he answered.

"But?" she prompted him tightly, hearing a qualification in his voice.

"But," he sighed, "what I really had in mind was marrying you."

Devon pulled away from him to get a better look at his eyes. Shock jolted through her. "Marry me? You told me you never wanted to get married again."

"So I changed my mind. Being without you these last four weeks gave me a lot of time to think. I love you, Devon. I don't need any escape clauses so that I can take my money and run if something goes wrong between us."

Wild firecrackers went off inside her again, but now they weren't born of anger. A thunderous euphoria crashed through her. "Nothing will go wrong," she answered confidently.

"What does that mean? That's not an answer. Don't start that again."

Another grin touched her lips. "It means yes. Yes, I'll marry you." She rushed on before a smile could claim his lips. "On one condition."

"Are we back to giving all my money away to charity again?"

Devon shook her head, unable to keep from laughing. "Nothing so serious as that. It's just that I refuse to become a professional socialite. I want to keep my catering business. See what you got yourself into when you found someone who didn't want you for your money? I won't be supported. I love what I do for a living."

Clay finally grinned. "That's easy enough to live with. It sure beats the hell out of giving my money to the S.P.C.A."

They smiled at each other in silence for a moment before she reached out to take his hand. "Come on," she said softly. "We've got some people to get rid of so that we can . . . uh, talk all night."

"Or whatever."

"Or whatever," she agreed happily. She got to her feet, then looked down at him. "Oh, by the way. There's something else I never told you."

He glanced at her sharply. "What?"

"I love you. Now. Present tense."

He stood up and pulled her into the circle of his arms. "I love you," he murmured. "Present tense. Now let's go get rid of those people."

They were halfway through the family room to the sliding glass doors before he paused. "Oh, by the way," he mimicked her. "There's something else I never told you."

Devon stopped dead in her tracks. "Yes?" she breathed.

"I knew."

"Knew what?"

"Well, actually, I suspected. That you were broke, that is."

"You've got to be kidding." She gaped at him. "Was it my excuses? Were they that transparent?"

Clay shook his head. "Nope. Your excuses were great, but you goofed up once, and when it happened, I couldn't forget it—even if I didn't want to admit to myself what it obviously meant."

Devon grabbed his arm. "What *what* meant?" she demanded. "Tell me! I put a lot of effort into keeping the truth from you!"

"All but once," he answered, grinning. "Do you remember the first time I called you? You pretended you were an answering machine."

Devon nodded slowly, coloring with embarrassment at the memory.

"And then you sneezed."

She suddenly understood. "And then I yelled downstairs for those people to stop fighting so that I could hear you."

"Bingo," he drawled, amusement in his eyes. "Sweetheart, professional socialites don't have neighbors arguing right outside their doors."

She forced herself to scowl at him. "One lousy goof. Big deal."

Clay sobered abruptly. "Actually, it was. It planted a seed in my brain that wouldn't let me rest. I ignored it. And because I wanted to ignore it so badly, I knew I loved you. I believed your excuses because I wanted to. It took me a long time to accept the fact that we didn't need them."

He pulled her against him again. Devon wrapped her arm around his waist, delighting in his nearness, as they walked outside onto the patio. "Come on," he finished. "Let's put an end to this damned party."

Fifteen faces gaped up at them as they joined the subdued crowd at the pool. Clay bent over and plucked two beers from the nearest cooler, then tossed one to Devon. Popping his open, he smiled mischievously at the people gathered around him. "Ladies and gentlemen," he began, "I'd like to propose a toast." He turned back to Devon, his eyes like green diamonds, his smile for her alone.

He lifted his beer toward her and never blinked when someone piped up quietly, "To what?"

His smile became conspiratorial and private. Devon shivered with happiness. "To the woman who's going to be my wife," he finished.

In the pandemonium that followed, no one noticed them join hands to go back inside.

An epic novel of exotic rituals
and the lure of the Upper Amazon

THE TAKERS RIVER OF GOLD

JERRY AND S.A. AHERN

THE TAKERS are the intrepid Josh Culhane and the seductive Mary Mulrooney. These two adventurers launch an incredible journey into the Brazilian rain forest. Far upriver, the jungle yields its deepest secret—the lost city of the Amazon warrior women!

THE TAKERS series is making publishing history. Awarded *The Romantic Times* first prize for High Adventure in 1984, the opening book in the series was hailed by *The Romantic Times* as "the next trend in romance writing and reading. Highly recommended!"

Jerry and S.A. Ahern have never been better!

TAK – 3

A Gold Eagle book from Worldwide, available now wherever Harlequin and Silhouette paperbacks are sold